Also by Ev Bishop

Bigger Things
Wedding Bands (River's Sigh B & B, Book 1)
Hooked (River's Sigh B & B, Book 2)
Spoons (River's Sigh B & B, Book 3)
Hook, Line & Sinker (River's Sigh B & B, Book 4)
Silver Bells (River's Sigh B & B, Book 5,
A Christmas novella)
New Year's Resolution: One To Keep
(A River's Sigh B & B novella)

Writing as Toni Sheridan
The Present
Drummer Boy

EV BISHOP

Silver Bells

River's Sigh B & B, Book 5
A Christmas Novella

SILVER BELLS
Book 5 in the River's Sigh B & B series
Copyright © 2018 Ev Bishop

Print Edition

Published by Winding Path Books

ISBN 978-1-77265-011-2

Cover image: Kimberly Killion / The Killion Group Inc.

To my plentiful siblings, with so much love.

Thank you for being nothing like Bryn's family and for making every holiday crazy, yes, but very fun!

Dear Reader,

I hope you enjoy *Silver Bells* as much as I enjoyed writing it. River's Sigh B & B is my own dream getaway. If you love visiting it as much as I do, you'll be happy to know you can "book" getaways with each of the other books in the series: *Wedding Bands*, *Hooked*, *Spoons*, *Hook, Line & Sinker*, and *One to Keep*.

Sign up for my newsletter to learn about upcoming books, and/or visit evbishop.com, find me on Facebook, follow my Tweets, or drop me a line at evbishop @evbishop.com. I'd love to hear from you! And on a similar note, reviews really help authors. If you would leave a few kind words on Amazon or anywhere else you like to hang out when your nose isn't in a book, I can't thank you enough.

Wishing you love, laughter and cozy nights,
☺ Ev

And now, happy reading . . .

Chapter 1

BRYN CHECKED THE ROAD BEHIND her in both side mirrors, then glanced in her rearview. Nothing but darkness beneath a churning blizzard of white. The view ahead was similarly void, but instead of streaming away from her in frantic billowing swirls, the heavy snow pushed toward her windshield in precise, mesmerizing lines. It reminded her of the opening crawl in the original Star Wars movie. She half-expected yellow lettering to appear. *A long time ago in a galaxy far, far away…*

Bryn's head bobbed—and the movement jolted her awake. She blinked hard and jerked the wheel, pulling her car back into what she hoped was her lane, though the centerline was impossible to see. Shoot. This no good. Steve, who was curled into a ball on the passenger seat, lifted his head and whined.

"I know, baby, I know. We're almost there." She wanted to give the little terrier's ears a reassuring scratch, but couldn't risk taking her concentration off the road again.

The problem was, they weren't close enough to

there yet. She hadn't made a hotel booking for Greenridge because she'd originally planned to push straight through, but even if she had, the small town was thirty to forty minutes away. Rupert, her destination, was three hours. The weather and road conditions had seriously slowed her progress.

Her Corolla's belly caught a thick ridge of ice and careened toward the snowbank on the highway's shoulder. Bryn fought the natural impulse to hit the brakes, knowing that would make the slide worse. In the nick of time, her wheels found purchase on the nearly indiscernible road. There was no good choice. She couldn't go any faster; the roads were too treacherous—but she couldn't go much slower either or her vehicle wouldn't have the power needed to push through the ever-deepening snow.

She turned off the old CD of Christmas tunes that had been crooning away the past hour and clicked the radio on, letting it search for the local station. A croak of broken voices and static met her ear. Rats. She was still out of the radio station's range.

A blast of wind slammed the side of her car and the whole vehicle shuddered. A snow-covered sign, marking what looked like a small rest area, appeared briefly, then was lost to the whirling white and deep shadows. It was increasingly impossible to see her surroundings. The clock on her dashboard read 8:14 p.m., but the sky was so dark and the traffic so sparse it seemed more like 2:00 *a.m.*

If her car kept high-centering on the unplowed highway—and if another vehicle happened by when she was out of control—it would spell disaster. Bryn decided to take the sign *as a sign* and turned on her signal light.

The rest area was to her immediate left now. She shoulder-checked yet again and pulled over as far as she could, noting with mild curiosity that the small clearing seemed to narrow at one end and become a one-lane road that wound away into nothingness.

She debated turning her four-way flashers on, but decided against it. She didn't want to attract attention to herself alone in the night. This way, if anyone passing by on the highway did happen to spot her dark vehicle, they'd just think some smart person had abandoned his or her car until the roads cleared.

She unclicked her seatbelt and reached into the backseat to retrieve her bulky winter coat from where it lay covering a pile of wrapped Christmas gifts and seasonal goodies. She also had a blanket, a candle and a lighter, water and nuts, and dog food. She'd wait until the storm lightened, dawn arrived and/or a plow truck came by, whichever came first. You can never be too prepared was her motto—something she found ironic, seeing as despite all her preparations for life, the things she wanted most seemed to allude her.

"Oh, come on," she muttered aloud. "Don't go there. Go to sleep. Take a nap."

Steve grunted from his seat as if in agreement.

3

But it was too late. Her brain, as ever, was already "there"—and the dangerous exhaustion that made her nod off on the road had evaporated. She felt wide awake. Great, just great. She'd known she'd have the blues this week. It almost couldn't be helped as she contemplated the solo road trip and the big family Christmas—but this? No, she hadn't even considered the possibility that she'd get stuck on a remote piece of road in the middle of nowhere with only herself and her spiraling thoughts for company.

She sighed and Steve echoed her, which made her smile the tiniest bit. At least she had Steve.

Yeah, Steve, a three-year-old mutt, your one—and only—true love.

Bryn's smile died.

Why did you even come? Every year you promise yourself you'll do your big visit in a less poignant season, yet every Christmas here you are…

It was funny to Bryn—and by "funny" she meant the furthest thing from—that even eight years since their divorce, her inner critic at its meanest still spoke in her ex-husband Brad's voice.

You know your family couldn't care less if you don't show up, right? Christmas is for people with kids, Bryn, not old maids.

Okay, so the last insult was something she used on herself, not really Brad's line, but the rest of the comment was pure him, verbatim. He'd said it one year when he wanted them to go to Mexico for

Christmas instead of to the big family gathering Bryn used to love so much.

Bryn reached into her glovebox and withdrew a package of bacon dog treats. Snoozing Steve was suddenly as awake as she was. She gave him one snack, then another, and put the package away.

"Of course, my family wants me there. They love me," she whispered defensively, feeling every bit of how pathetic she was: thirty-five years old, stranded alone in the dark in the boonies a week before Christmas, arguing with her long-gone ex that her mummy and daddy do so love her.

And they did—just maybe not quite as much as they loved her three sisters with their busy, happy hordes of kids and loyal husbands. Spinster Bryn, with her condo in an adults-only complex and full-time career focus, was out of the loop. It didn't matter that Bryn was a homebody, who loved to bake and cook and decorate, her mom and sisters acted like she had nothing in common with them, nothing to add or contribute to conversations…

"Of course, you 'love' to cook—because you don't have to, day in, day out," her sister Sasha had laughed at Thanksgiving once, when Bryn chimed in on a discussion about recipes and volunteered to head up the bulk of the cooking.

"It is different when you're cooking for a family instead of one person," Bryn's mom had agreed gently.

It was just one stupid exchange, but one of so many

similar ones over the years that it became symbolic to Bryn of all the ways she was the outsider, the odd woman out—barren and husbandless in her close-knit, progeny-producing family. It wasn't hard to pick out the instance of unintentional insensitivity that had hurt her most, however. Hands down it was when she'd broken the news to her mom and dad, still shattered and reeling from the unforeseen blow, that Brad was leaving her because she couldn't have kids and it was important to him to have his own biological children.

"I know it's hard, honey—but it's nature, you know? Men want to leave a legacy."

That had been her mother's idea of sympathy. *That.* What about Bryn's nature? What about her disappointment? She had always, always, *always* wanted kids. Some people weren't sure or could go either way, especially when they were young, but all Bryn's fantasies had centered around house and home: one husband to love her for all her days—and a handful of kids. It was embarrassing how traditional and mumsy she was at heart—and she'd tried hard to downplay it at university. Having or not having children was supposed to be a rational, intellectual decision these days, not a craving from some deep, ancient part of your body and blood, not taken as a given conclusion, the way you expect your arms and legs to work, your heart to thump, your blood to automatically pump. But that's how she'd been when she thought about the children she'd have—that they would just... *be*. The idea of anything else had never occurred to her.

Bryn tucked her coat around her more securely and reclined her seat. Although she hadn't been parked for long, the windshield was completely covered in snow. Bryn sighed again; Steve sighed again.

Just for kicks, Bryn turned the car on briefly and let the wipers clear her front and back windows—not that there was anything to see. She rechecked the radio—still nothing. Powered her cell phone on—no service, but she hadn't been expecting any.

Her head was loud and whiney and sad and she was sick of herself. Outside the car, the silence was a heavy, breathing presence.

"Your life is lovely," she whispered. "You're healthy. You have friends who love you. You have work that matters to you and that supplies all your needs. No one gets everything."

Her gratitude wasn't feigned. It really wasn't. It was just that Christmas, the season that celebrated new life and family from its very roots, was a raw reminder of things she didn't have but had always longed for.

A distant rumbling registered in her consciousness. Something about it put her on alert, though she couldn't say what exactly. Maybe just that until now the whole world had been devoid of sound, muffled in snow, like she was the sole inhabitant of the isolated road she found herself on.

The noise grew louder and louder—became the

roar of a big diesel engine.

Bryn cracked her door and poked her head out, peering into the dizzying white. She saw high beams and caught the glare of a chrome grill. Then a Dodge truck, black as the night, hurtled past, pushing snow and sending huge plumes of exhaust into the frigid air. The driver noticed the sharp curve looming ahead, too late. The angry red glow of brake lights split the darkness. Bryn had time for only the briefest thought. That truck's going too fast. It's going to—

A spinning carnival ride of lights lit up the night before her shocked eyes. The truck spun donut after donut, totally out of control. There was no screech of metal or rubber on cement, just a heavy whirring shush as the vehicle whooshed through the snow. Then it disappeared off the side of the road in a cloud of powder.

Into a ditch? Into the river that ran parallel to this stretch of highway in places? Bryn hated that she didn't know exactly where she was on the road. She had an idea, but any truly familiar landmarks were obliterated by the night and the white.

A flood of adrenalin made her nauseous. She *thought* she could see lights level with the highway, glowing almost yellow, from beneath a layer of snow. So not in the river then—please God *not*, she prayed.

Bryn sat back in her car and shut her door, fretting. She should check on the person or persons in the truck. What if someone was hurt? She knew first aid. But what if the vehicle's occupants were as crazy and potentially dangerous as the way they drove? Still, she couldn't just leave them. She'd bring her phone and as she approached, she'd speak into it, like she'd been able to reach 9-1-1 and there was someone on the way. Even the biggest psycho, upon crashing his truck in a storm, would probably have bigger things on his mind than attacking a would-be helper.

Not completely happy with her decision, but knowing she'd never be able to live with herself if someone was hurt, then worsened or died when she could've helped, Bryn climbed out of her car. She bundled herself up in her long down jacket and fastened its hood securely under her chin. Then she wrapped a scarf around her face, leaving only her eyes peeking out. She put her key fob in her pocket and zipped it up, then, for added precaution, took her extra key out of a hidden change drawer in the car and put it in the ignition.

"Hold tight," she told Steve. "I'll be right back."

She closed her door, careful not to lock it, and waded through the deep snow toward the buried truck.

Chapter 2

"YOU *IDIOT*," SEAN SEETHED, BANGING his palms against his steering wheel in frustrated fury. He'd been speeding, he admitted it. Worse, he'd been totally distracted—and by stupid woe-is-me stuff. He hadn't even clued in to the fact he was in trouble until it was too late and he'd lost control and couldn't get it back. "Story of my life," he grumbled.

He pressed the gas pedal. The engine revved, but there was no forward movement. His tires didn't even spin.

He cut the engine, stretched his neck and rubbed his head, then felt along each of his arms and pushed at his ribs. He didn't seem injured. That was good at least.

Outside his truck's cab, the wind shrieked and whistled. There was nothing to see for miles that he could tell—just a blinding, dizzying flurry of white and swirling darkness. He contemplated what to do next. He figured he was forty or fifty kilometers from Greenridge, way too far to walk. He rested his fore-arms on his steering wheel, then dropped his head.

This was great, just great. A Christmas holiday to top all the rotten ones of the past five years, and that was saying something, considering how low he'd felt during some of them. Here he'd been congratulating himself on facing the storm strongly and head-on, the way he should be facing the rest of his life, and this was the good it did him.

Oh, come on. Was he seriously trying to say his stupid driving wasn't his own fault?

No, he wasn't. Being all angst-ridden and depressed by the Christmas spirit tinkling here, there and everywhere, reminding him of his loneliness, was no reason to drive irresponsibly.

He straightened abruptly, undid his seatbelt, and rummaged for his coat. A jumble of stuff had hit the floor when the truck made impact with whatever had stopped it. He supposed he should consider himself lucky—he could've gone off into the river and that would've been the end of him—but he couldn't scrounge up gratitude, only relief. It kind of reminded him of his relationship with Gemma, actually—or his *ex*-relationship with Gemma, that is. He should be thankful that they weren't still together, that she'd "cut him loose" to quote her compassionate break up speech—but he couldn't quite muster it.

It wasn't that he was still hung up on Gemma. Yes, she'd only ended it officially six months ago, but he had finally learned his lesson. She didn't love him. In fact, she had never loved him, at least not according to his "old-fashioned ideals" about love anyway. Leave it to Gemma to think having ideals was old-fashioned, an insult, not something good or worth striving for.

The end of their ten-year relationship had shocked him by not being a lot more difficult—or any less lonely—than being with her. Often it was even a relief. He was no longer yanked back and forth, caught in a cycle of being dumped because he "wasn't working for her"—always quickly followed by some variation of, "I'm so sorry. Please come back. This time I mean it. I can't live without you."

Other times, like now, he was sad about what might have been, about losing what he'd always wanted and hoped they were working toward, however inconsistently. Her confession that she'd had another guy on the side for "a while"—some douchebag named Marcus—was the last straw, though. Even Sean wasn't a big enough sucker to keep fooling himself then.

It hurt that Gemma had cheated on him, but more than that, it made Sean angry. At himself. Why on earth was he so arrogant and naive to think he'd change her? That she'd suddenly genuinely want the things he did? Why had he been so dumb and unable to see through her? He'd been a fool, for not being happy alone, for wishing there was something more for him, for being the kind of sap who always just wanted a family and kids.

His hands finally landed on his jacket. It was soaking wet for some reason. Sean held it up to his face in the truck's dark cab and sniffed. No odor that he could detect, but the wetness felt kind of sticky. A light went on—but only in his head, of course. The case of soda he'd brought with him must've burst. *Awesome.*

The wind died down and, for the time being at least, all was still. Sean decided he'd better brave the elements in his long sleeve T-shirt and sweater before the storm kicked up again. He needed to see if digging his truck out himself was even a remote possibility, or if he was going to be stuck until morning.

Just as he was about to open his door, he froze. Something—someone?—was moving in the thick darkness. The muffled shuffling sound came closer to the truck—and closer. What would be out in this weather? Nothing good. He would've seen or heard if a cop car or some other vehicle had driven up.

Thump, thump. Sean jumped. Someone was banging the side of the truck, near the hood. He wasn't imagining it. Thump, thump. Were they trying to feel along the body of the vehicle? Had someone witnessed him go off the road? There was another thump—at his door now. Sean stared out the window and his eyes locked on a faceless, hooded specter—a slightly darker shadow in a night of shadows. *It's a person, just a person in a big coat.* Despite knowing that was true, his heart still hammered extra fast.

The faceless entity leaned closer and its shadowy outline grew more pronounced. The handle clicked, but the door didn't open. Sean hadn't hit unlock yet.

"Hello?" a tentative, feminine voice called. "Are you okay? Is anybody hurt?"

Sean's anger was instantaneous and irrational— maybe he had bashed his head, after all. "I'm fine," he roared, throwing open the door. "I just put myself off the road like a big jerk."

His rescuer made a startled sound and rushed sideways, barely avoiding being hit by the door. His truck must've landed in a drift because the snow was literally up past the woman's waist. She was wading, not walking. "Oh, well… good then—that you're fine, not that you, uh, went off the road."

Sean scanned the darkness, but there was nothing to see but the black silhouette of the forest's tree line and mounds and mounds of heavy—and still accumulating—snow. He strained his ears, but there was nothing to hear but silence and the slightly husky breathing of the woman.

"Who are you?" he asked.

"Bryn. Bryn Hale. I was parked in what I thought was a rest area when you—"

Sean held up his hand. He didn't want to hear her interpretation of his carelessness. "You have a car?"

"Yes, but it's not handling the snow very well."

"I could drive it out."

"No, you couldn't, Mr.—?" This Bryn Hale woman's voice was firm, and Sean was unsure whether she meant he would be *unable* to drive the vehicle because of the weather conditions, or if she was saying he *wasn't allowed* to drive it because, well, look at him— not exactly an ode to driving ability.

"Carson," Sean supplied. "Sean Carson."

The woman turned away. "I'll let you be then, Mr. Carson. I just wanted to make sure you were all right."

Sean hesitated, then called, "Wait. What are you going to do?"

"Car camp until morning. I recommend you do the same." She was making decent time now that she could retrace the rough path she'd forged through the snow during her approach. Her breath made little white puffs in the darkness.

Sean turned back to his truck, grabbed his backpack, then locked the door and shoved his keys into his jeans' pocket. "Do you know where we are?" he called after her.

"About half an hour east of Greenridge."

"And you're traveling this highway alone at night in this weather?"

The woman stopped and half turned back. "Um, yes." Her face was still invisible, but her tone suggested she thought him a bit unstable. "And so are you. What's your point?"

Sean hadn't intended to be sexist, but realized it was probably how he sounded. There was no point, however, in lecturing the stranger about how he'd been raised by a strong single mom and a sister tough enough to take on anyone.

"And correction, I'm not actually alone. I left my

good boy Steve in my vehicle." The wind screeched in renewed fury, muffling her next line. It sounded like she said, "He's, ah, terrific."

Her "good boy Steve"—who's *ah, terrific*? And this Bryn woman was acting like he was the unhinged person in this situation? Poor Steve, whoever he was. He didn't think he was a child—she didn't seem overly concerned about getting back to him—but if he was her partner? Yikes, he felt bad for the guy.

As if sensing Sean's unspoken critique, Bryn's head bobbed in what appeared to be a solid up and down glance. "Correction two, you're traveling *this* highway, *alone at night*—and *you* don't even have a decent jacket?"

Sean had a perfectly good winter coat, thank you very much. It just was inconveniently drenched in soda at the moment. He didn't figure either point bore mentioning, however. He slung his pack over his shoulder as he recalled something she'd said earlier, something curious.

"You said you'd parked in what you *thought* was a rest area. If it's not one, what is it?"

Chapter 3

BRYN AND SEAN STOOD AT the edge of the highway, a good distance from his truck and a fair way from her car, looking up at a huge carved sign. Tin-capped cedar mountains shone silver, and a rising sun glowed in the dim beam of a snow encrusted light at the sign's base. A flourish of text announced River's Sigh B & B, and an arrow directed them into the woods, down the winding path Bryn had noticed earlier.

She tugged her scarf, though it still covered most of her face, higher yet. Not because she was cold, but because... oh, man, was she actually blushing? What a freak! Yet she couldn't help it. Back at the snow-buried truck in the deep shadows—then trudging in front of him through the snow—Bryn had mistaken slightly snarly Sean Carson for some curmudgeonly old man. Here and now, the dim yellow light told a different story. Correction three... (And good grief, how embarrassing were her anal-retentive corrections? She could kick herself!) Sean wasn't old—or not much older than her anyway. And he was, er, surprisingly—cheek warmingly, stutter inducingly—good looking.

He had tousled black hair, lovely, touchable look-ing olive skin, and a couple days' worth of stubble on a strong chin that Bryn wanted to rub herself up and down on—Holy Hannah, what is wrong with you!? her brain intoned.

"I'm a desperate loser and it's showing?" Bryn muttered back under her breath—then realized to her horror she'd whispered the words aloud.

"What?" Sean looked away from the sign and stepped closer.

"Nothing," Bryn said loudly and clearly. Kill me now, she thought.

Was it her imagination or did his pale blue eyes, so striking against his swarthy skin, crease with amuse-ment? If he had heard and was laughing at her, nothing in his tone gave him away.

"Your car's over there somewhere?" he asked, jerking his chin in the direction of her invisible vehi-cle.

She nodded.

"If you're okay with leaving it overnight, why don't we check out this River's Sigh place?"

Bryn looked at Sean—felt ridiculously warm again—then glanced toward the area where she knew her Corolla sat parked. It was well away from the road, safe from any passing snow plows. She studied the spot in the turnoff that narrowed into what must be the B & B's driveway. It would definitely be more com-fortable than spending a night cramped in her vehicle.

How far could it be?

"Okay," she said slowly. "Just let me get Steve."

Sean followed her to her car and waited patiently as she clicked on the interior light and deliberated whether to bring her suitcase or just an overnight bag. She decided on the latter. She didn't want to lug a suitcase for who knew how many miles. She added her purse to her overnight bag, then grabbed Steve's blue blanket from the back, along with his leash, and whistled. He jumped out immediately, disappeared into the snow—then scrambled back into the car.

"Come on, silly. I know you hate the cold, but you won't melt. I promise." Steve shot her a side-eyed glance that suggested he didn't believe her one bit, but did as asked and hopped out onto the ground near Sean's feet.

"Steve's a dog!" Sean exclaimed.

"Uh—yeah?" Bryn flicked the lights off, locked her car and turned, sounding amused. "That's what a terrier is."

"I thought you were talking about some guy who was *ah, terrific*."

Bryn giggled. She couldn't help it. "That I also referred to as my 'good boy'? Poor man—if he existed."

Steve jumped around Sean's feet, disappearing and reappearing with each hop in in the fluffy snow.

"So there's no sad, infantilized man in your life, just Steve who you talk to like a person? I've heard of crazy cat ladies, and I have to admit, being a crazy dog lady is way better."

The inexplicable fluttery (stupid!) feeling that had been tormenting Bryn cooled. Just because she revealed in passing that she was single and just because she had a small dog that she obviously loved, this man thought he knew something about her? You could adore your pet *and* be happily married *and* have kids. Just look at all her annoying sisters!

"Did I say something wrong?" Sean asked a second later.

"No, no, of course not." He had, but it wasn't his fault. She apparently sent out a vibe like an invisible beacon—spinster for life. Even a gorgeous stranger in the middle of the night in almost pitch darkness picked up on it.

"If we're going to do this," she added, "we should get going. It's getting late and we have no idea how far it is."

Sean took the blanket from her, crouched down and coaxed Steve into his arms. Then he glanced up. "It's going to be hard on the little guy, pushing through all that snow. I figured we could take turns carrying him and letting him walk."

All Bryn's warm feelings flooded back. Dumb, dumb, dumb—but again she had no control over it. Sean may have written her off as some gooney old dog lady, but underneath her layers of down and wool, she was just a girl, standing in front of a boy.

"You *seriously* need help," she whispered as she started toward the opening in the tree line.

"Sorry, I didn't catch that. What?" Sean called.

Chapter 4

THE TREK TO RIVER'S SIGH B & B was both worse and better than Sean had been expecting. Obviously, the establishment did their own snow removal, hence their turnoff and driveway being passable, at least compared to the highway, but it was a much longer walk than he'd expected. *That*—the long walk—was the better part. He wasn't appreciating his snow-filled boots or the white stuff accumulating on his clothes—he and Bryn were going to look like White Walkers from *Game of Thrones* when they were done—but he was enjoying funny, quirky Bryn's company very much.

Back at her car when she was collecting overnight things and first introduced him to Steve, she'd seemed a little snippy about his dog lady comment. Maybe she liked cats too and found him mildly offensive? Either way, he'd worried that conversation would be non-existent or stilted as they walked—but nothing could have been further from the truth.

The first hundred or so paces along the unfamiliar road were intimidating, but the heaviest of the clouds moved on and the snow fell softer. Every so often the moon peeked through, reflecting off each snow-covered tree and log, bathing their surroundings in a strangely luminous blue-white light. As agreed, they took turns carrying Steve and letting him walk inter-mittently. The small dog bounded rabbit-like through the deep snow, looking back at them from time to time as if to make sure they were appreciating how athletic and amazing he was. They both laughed every time.

They were surprised to find out they lived in the same small city, six hours from Greenridge. Sean planned to share Christmas with a friend who had relocated to Greenridge a few years back. Bryn told him of her family plans in Rupert, another three hours further along the highway.

They talked about movies and books. She devoured fiction of all kinds, but especially loved contemporary and regency romances. He had to pry it out of her. She kept insisting she didn't really have favorite genres—but she did and he felt oddly satisfied at having gotten her to trust him with it.

When he told her he preferred non-fiction, she chuckled. "You're such a *guy*."

"Thanks for noticing," he replied, making her laugh again. He loved her laugh—and how she laughed so often, a sweet tinkling sound, bell-like in the still, cold air.

Under duress (okay... "duress" was a strong word; she'd only thrown one snow ball) he confessed his own dirty secret—that he read self-help. Then Netflix somehow came up and they discovered they were both series junkies—and binged on the same shows, loving crime and suspense, zombies and sci-fi.

He discovered she worked in a group home, providing care for adults with special needs. She seemed genuinely interested when he mentioned he owned and ran an event planning company.

Earlier, he never could have predicted how his evening would go from nightmarish to dreamlike in such a short time—but that's how it felt: like a happy dream. It really seemed as if the bitterest part of the storm had ended. The moon no longer peeked at them. It burst free of the brooding clouds entirely, huge and bright. Under its kiss, the snow-laden evergreens shone silver and the road before them was transformed into a shining white ribbon. It was like walking in a living, breathing Christmas card.

Bryn kept herself well wrapped, which made total sense, considering the weather and the temperature, but Sean found himself torn. He wanted to see the face of this woman he was finding so attractive. He already knew he wouldn't be disappointed. He liked *her* and that wouldn't change—but he was curious. And what if she was much, much older than he was—or, worse, horribly younger? He wasn't into that. During their first exchange or two, he'd pegged her as older. Now, especially with her Netflix obsession, she seemed younger—and her voice was young.

"So how old are you anyway?" he finally asked,

feeling awkward for the first time since they started their journey.

She gave him what he imagined would've been a sharp look except it's hard to do anything sharply when your head is a mass of wrapped blue fluff. "Thirty-five. Why?"

He shrugged. Why did she sound almost defensive? "No reason, really. I'm thirty-eight."

Eventually their conversation waned as they continued slogging through the snow. The walk was starting to feel *too* long. Sean wondered if he'd gotten her to join him on some fool's errand. Steve seemed cold and tired and no longer wanted to walk at all, whining if they tried to put him down.

"Maybe we misinterpreted the sign," Bryn worried aloud, giving voice to his silent concerns. "Maybe it was for something further along the highway. Maybe this is just an old logging road or something—or maybe there was another turn off on this road, but we missed it somehow."

"Yeah, maybe." Sean looked around. There were still no signs of human life or activity, except—"The road is plowed though. It's filling in, yes, but it *was* plowed—and fairly recently."

Bryn's tone brightened immediately. "You're right, so we must be headed to somewhere. I hope it's not some summer only place—and that they have rooms available."

Sean hadn't even considered that it might be a seasonal B & B. "So what should we do? Do you want to keep going for a bit, or turn back?"

"Umm, maybe keep going for another ten minutes, then re-evaluate?"

"Sounds good."

A few minutes later, Steve struggled in Sean's arms and let out an anxious yip. Sean handed Steve to Bryn, but the dog wouldn't settle.

"Shhh," Bryn said, wrapping the terrier more snugly and covering his small head with the corner of his blue blanket. Then she inhaled sharply. "Oh, that's why you're excited. Good boy!"

Steve's blanketed form wiggled as if in agreement, then stilled, and Sean laughed—as much at the exchange between Bryn and Steve, as from relief. The snow beyond a nearing bend in the road sparkled with soft red, green and blue light. It could only mean one thing: a Christmas tree.

No words were needed. He and Bryn simultaneously picked up their pace and soon found themselves in another Christmas card worthy picture: one featuring a cozy house, its windows aglow with candlelight, surrounded by snow that looked almost blue in the deep shadows. Tiny white lights decorated a copse of birch trees and a massive spruce gleamed cheerily, decked out in blue, green, red and yellow bulbs.

"It's so pretty," Bryn breathed.

They made their way across a large circle-shaped parking area, and Sean tried to be reassured by a variety of snowy lumps that had to be vehicles. That many trucks and cars must mean there were guests— but then again, it was deeply quiet and, while, yes, the windows on the main house were glowing, the office was dark. At the very least, they'd be disturbing the owners during their personal time.

"Here goes nothing." Sean climbed three stairs to stand on the deck that wrapped the full perimeter of the house. Bryn followed, holding a sleeping Steve close. Sean knocked three times on the bright blue door in front of him. The holly wreath adorning it rustled cheerily.

Just as he was about to rap once more, the door opened. A stunning blonde, more Hollywood than backwoods BC, appeared. "Yes?" she said.

Sean motioned at Bryn who stood slightly behind him, holding blanket-wrapped Steve tightly. "I'm sorry to bother you so late, but we've been travelling all day and now the storm's gotten the best of us. I know it's last minute, but do you by any chance have room—"

He was cut off by a chortle of laughter. "Stop, no—you have to be kidding!" The blonde disappeared into the house, and they heard her calling, "Jo, Jo— come quick. You're never going to believe who's at the door and what they want."

"Um," Bryn whispered almost inaudibly at Sean's back. "Should we be afraid? Maybe we've stumbled upon Little House in the Zombie Woods."

Chapter 5

SEAN LAUGHED AT BRYN'S JOKE, too busy enjoying the seductive heat wafting from the open door and the mouth-watering aroma of garlic and fresh, buttery bread to feel wary. His stomach growled rudely and a huge shiver ran through him. That—his deep chill— almost made him worry. He'd gotten a lot colder during their walk than he'd thought he would. He just hadn't noticed it earlier because he'd been so busy enjoying Bryn's company.

"Is anyone else going to come to the door, do you think?" Bryn asked. "And if not, do you think we can make off with some of whatever's making that glorious smell?"

"I'm game to try if you are," Sean said as another pretty woman appeared, this one with long wild reddish-gold curls. She was flanked by a tall dark-haired guy about his own age.

"I'm sorry," she said. "You just met my sister Sam. She was reading the Nativity story to her granddaughter and thought your timing and wording was a hilarious coincidence." The woman must've realized that Sean was struggling to keep up. "I'm sorry," she repeated. "I'm Jo. This is my husband Callum. We own River's Sigh. Sam was saying you need a place to stay tonight?"

"Yes, absolutely."

"You're in luck. A cabin literally just became available. It was booked, but the folks who reserved it called barely twenty minutes ago to say they can't make it. The roads are too bad. The cabin doesn't come with a crib, but my niece has a playpen that might do nicely and she doesn't mind lending."

"I'll grab it for you," the husband—Callum—volunteered, but Sean was still focused on the first part of Jo's information.

"Only one room?" he asked.

Bryn stepped closer to the door and sounded equally, if not more, confused. "A crib?"

Jo and Callum exchanged a quick look, then glanced at Sean and Bryn again. "Um, Sam said… Aren't you a couple, stranded by weather, needing a room for you and your small baby?"

Sean cleared his throat, then got Sam's joke. Bryn was so covered in snow, she appeared to be wearing robes—and Steve, cuddled close to her chest, could only be described as swaddled. He darted a look at Bryn, but only her gray eyes were visible above her frosty scarf and they gave nothing away. Maybe she didn't find it funny.

Sean shook his head. "I should've been clearer,

sorry. We're here together, but we're not *together-together*—and we're not traveling because of a census or anything."

Bryn snorted softly behind him and his lip twitched. So she did find the situation at least a little comical, after all. Why was that such a big deal to him, that she wouldn't be offended?

"We just walked in from the highway—"

Steve chose that moment to wake up and stretch. The blanket twisted dramatically and he let out a weird moaning sound.

Callum was visibly startled. Jo looked surprised too, and a grizzled white, brown and gray mutt appeared from behind her legs.

"It's—this—is Steve. He's a dog, not a baby," Bryn supplied. The blanket vibrated some more, and Steve popped his head out.

Jo laughed almost as hard as Sam had when she first opened the door. "Ah, and that explains Hoover's interest."

"I guess this means I don't have to traipse through the snow with a playpen," Callum said.

"True," Jo agreed. "But they're probably starved. Are you starved?" She didn't wait for a reply. "Do you mind packing them a dinner, sweetie?"

"Absolutely." Callum disappeared before Sean or Bryn could politely pretend that they couldn't possibly take their food.

"It's just leftovers—we had a big family do tonight—but everything was cooked in a restaurant grade kitchen, if you're hungry."

"It smells amazing," Sean said quickly.

"Yeah, well, I wouldn't want you guys to feel like you had to sneak in just to get food."

Bryn groaned. "I was only joking, I promise."

"I know that," Jo said merrily. She grabbed a coat off a hook near the door, then slipped into knee high fur-lined boots. "Let's get you guys settled... Wait a minute. You said you're not together? As in you're not a couple? You mean you want separate accommodations?"

"Yes, please," Sean and Bryn said as one.

Jo was on the deck now, about to head down the stairs to the parking lot. She looked back and her eyes were big and regretful in the porch light. "I'm really sorry. We only have the one cabin available for tonight and it's a bachelor—just one bed, I'm afraid. There is a small couch, but..."

Sean looked at Bryn and felt terrible. This was all his fault. She'd dragged herself out of her warm vehicle where she'd been all set to sit out the storm because of his dumb ass driving—and then he'd convinced her to spend almost two hours trekking through the snow. He knew what he had to do, and could only hope he could beg a bit of dinner before he headed back to his lonely cold vehicle.

"It's okay," he said. "Bryn, you take the room. I'll go back to my truck. I'll be fine."

Callum appeared in a navy peacoat and thick gray muffler. He was carrying an insulated bag that looked impossibly full for just two people. Sean's stomach growled louder and Bryn peered at him over her scarf, which had thawed a little in the heat from the doorway. "No, no, don't be silly. We'll take the room, Jo. Thank you."

"Are you sure?" Sean didn't know if he was flattered or terrified for this woman who approached stranded vehicles in the dead of night and offered to share rooms with virtual strangers.

Bryn nodded. Jo and Callum remained inert, waiting on his reply it seemed.

"Well, if you're really sure—"

"I am."

"Then I'll take the couch."

"Absolutely, you will," Bryn said, but there was humor in her voice. "*Ah-terrific* and I need all the space we can get."

Sean was feeling gratitude now, not just relief, as he, Bryn and Steve followed Jo and Callum back into the night.

Chapter 6

ALTHOUGH THE WORST OF THE storm was over, heavy wet snow continued to fall. Bryn thought Sean looked frozen, almost snowman like—although, admittedly, oxymoron aside, he made a pretty hot snowman.

Trudging along, she could only imagine how awful she'd look when she finally got out of her snow clothes. Nothing special on her best day, exhaustion and exposure to extreme weather were not going to do her dishwater dull hair, blah eyes and pale complexion any favors—not that it should matter. Who cared what she looked like?

She knew the answer too well, even though it was utterly humiliating: she did. There was no way, of course, that Sean would be interested in geeky, weird her... but it would be nice if he wasn't horrified the first time he laid eyes on her.

As Jo and Callum moved them along the well-groomed trail, describing and naming each cabin they passed, Bryn wondered if she'd lost her mind. What had she been thinking, inviting Sean to stay the night in a tiny, one-bed cabin with her? He was a stranger. It didn't matter how they'd seemed to click during their long walk.

Yet it was the middle of night, the poor guy's truck was toast, and the temperature would only keep dropping until morning. She was being a good Samaritan.

Uh huh. Right. She just hoped he didn't get the wrong idea and think she was hitting on him. *Was* she hitting on him? Errgh, if he gave her some variation of the "you're a nice person, but" speech, it would be beyond embarrassing. What was the least awkward way for her to open—and close—the subject before he could?

Steve wriggled in her arms and she set him down. He immediately peed then pranced down the trail in front of them.

Sean said something that she didn't quite hear.

"Pardon?"

"Oh…" He sounded as self-conscious as she felt. "I only said it's crazy pretty here, hey?"

"Yeah," she said, and it really was: all snowy trees, twinkly lights and tiny picturesque cabins, most slumbering away in the night, but here or there, one or two with softly glowing windows.

"Here we are." Jo stopped suddenly on the trail before them. "We call it Trout. It was just finished up a few weeks ago—two nights before the first snowfall, thankfully." She waved her arm at the tiny cabin. Its porch light was on, illuminating a cranberry red door decorated with a huge wreath of soft pine and ivy. Antique silver bells—real ones—hung at the bottom of the wreath and clanged softly as Jo opened the door. She clicked on an interior light, then handed them the keys.

"No cell service here," she said, "and there's no landline or Internet hooked up in this cabin yet. Please feel free to use our office phone or Wi-Fi tomorrow."

"And this should hold you over food-wise," Callum added, passing the bag he carried to Sean. "Breakfast is served between eight and ten, see you then."

Sean and Bryn thanked their hosts and said good night, then Jo and Callum headed back to the trail. Bryn whistled for Steve. He bounded over and zipped into the cabin. Obviously, *he* wasn't feeling awkward at all. She and Sean followed him in, and Bryn wondered if Sean, like her, felt ill at ease. Probably not. He probably entertained one night stands all the time—which made her cringe. What if he thought that's what she had in mind? I mean, she'd clearly said he was getting the couch, but her tone had been kind of jokey…

You're being nuts, she told herself. Sean has acted like nothing but a genuinely decent guy—once he got his initial anger and surprise out of the way at the scene of the accident anyway.

Recognizing the truth in her words, Bryn calmed. She set her overnight bag down on a cedar bench in the small entrance way and pulled off her boots. Before she got a chance to remove her jacket and scarf, however, Sean stopped her with a hand on her arm.

"What?" she asked.

"I just wanted to thank you again, for letting me crash here with you. I'm exhausted."

She nodded. "I bet you are. You've had a rough night. I'm sorry."

"You, of all people, don't need to apologize to me."

She had been sympathizing not apologizing, but that wasn't what struck her oddly. "Me, *of all people—* what does that mean?"

"That I owe you an apology. I was a rude jerk when you knocked on my truck door. I was startled—"

"And in a bit of shock from going off the road. It's okay."

"No, it's not okay. I was furious with myself for driving like an ass—and embarrassed. I took it out on you at first. I'm sorry."

"No apology necessary."

"That's just the thing. I *do* feel it's necessary. You were very gracious and kind to risk seeing if I needed help—not to mention brave—so thank you."

Bryn shrugged, but couldn't deny that his words lit a happy little glow in her belly. Anybody would've done what she'd done, but it was nice to be appreciated. She unwrapped her scarf and hung it to dry on a hook by the door, then unzipped her long coat and put it away as well.

When she turned to see where Steve had gotten to, she didn't spot her dog immediately—but she did catch Sean's look. He was staring intently and seemed mildly shocked or confused by something. When her eyes met his, he quickly glanced away.

Bryn looked down at herself. "What?"

Sean shrugged.

"No, seriously, *what*?"

"It's just that… you're beautiful. I already knew I liked you, but I wasn't expecting…" He gestured with his hands, like he was presenting something—presenting *her*.

A surprised smile bloomed across Bryn's face before she could stop it, and tingling heat in her cheeks told her she'd just let Sean know in red technicolor how flattered his words made her feel.

But she was not beautiful; she was plain—and he was kind. Flustered, Bryn said the first thing to pop into her head, other than *you're the one who's beautiful*. "You're dripping on the floor."

Sean looked down. "Oh, I really am."

She nodded. The cozy warmth of the cabin was thawing his snow-logged sweater. As if cued by the droplets forming a small puddle on the stone tiles, Sean quaked in a full body shiver.

"Good grief, you're freezing to death."

"Well, *to death* is a bit of an exaggeration—or so I hope, anyway." His eyes crinkled charmingly. He really did have the cutest smile, and it was lovely to get to see it in full light. Sap, sap, sap! Bryn told herself.

"You're not one of those macho types who acts all stupidly tough at the expense of their health and well-being, are you?"

Why did she always resort to being such a snarky bag when she felt uncomfortable?

Sean's smile slid from his mouth, but continued to twinkle in his eyes. "Oh, I'm one of those macho types all right—the macho-est, in fact," he mock growled. "But I am pretty badly chilled."

Bryn giggled, then clamped back the sound. There was no way he was flirting with her. She was imagining things. "What you need is a warm soak. Let me see if this place has a bathtub, and I'll run you one."

The gentle teasing look fell from Sean's face and was replaced by a slightly confused, quizzical expression.

Good lord, why was she such a weirdo? Like a grown man couldn't fill his own bathtub? He would for sure think she was either hitting on him—suggesting a little tub action for two—which was mortifying appealing, she admitted—or that she was being some bizarre meddling wannabe mother figure—or a strange combo of both. Ugh!

The main part of the cabin was open concept and floored with multi-hued tiles that reminded Bryn of river stones, and there was a living room visually set apart from the rest of the space by a roomy square of warm plank flooring. Beyond that lay two closed doors. Bryn grabbed her night bag and fled past a beautiful slab of wood that formed an eating bar across from a small L-shaped kitchen nook before Sean could say a word. She peeked in one door and shut it, then peeked in another. Bingo.

She started the tub as promised.

"Are you allergic to eucalyptus?" she called.

"Um… no."

His tone definitely suggested confusion. He was probably wondering what kind of lunatic he'd accidentally got himself locked up with for the night. Why did she go into extreme nurturer mode when she was nervous? Ah well, it was too late now—and at least the bath would be good for him, might even stave off getting a cold.

"Um," he repeated when she popped out of the bathroom a moment later and told him it should be all ready for him. "Thank you?"

Bryn's face burned as he headed into the steamy bathroom with his backpack and the impact of the situation hit her. He was going to take a bath—because she hadn't left him any choice in the matter. Yikes.

Her dismay over her embarrassing tendency to fall into caregiver mode—an occupational hazard—faded quickly, however, as her imagination kicked in. *Sean Carson soaking in a fragrant, bubble-filled tub*. The image removed all traces of chill left from their sojourn through the freezing dark. In fact, she practically needed a fan.

What was wrong with her? She wasn't usually such a bundle of uncontrolled hormones.

She went to the stove and turned the oven to a low heat, then unpacked the food Callum and Jo had provided. Her stomach rumbled as delicious smell after delicious smell teased her senses. After checking each aluminum container's contents—two massive pieces of lasagna in one, garlicky ribs in the other—she placed them in the oven to stay warm. Then she peeked at the other plastic tubs and felt herself salivate. Assorted olives and cheeses in one partitioned box. A whipped cream and chocolate dessert of some kind in another. Foil-wrapped garlic bread that seemed homemade. She added the bread to the oven.

The hearty comfort food felt like exactly what the doctor ordered. She felt weirdly excited.

A splashing sound from the bathroom tickled her ear—followed by a gusty sigh of contentment that made her body tingle again. At least Sean didn't sound like he was resenting the forced bath.

The meal was too nice to eat from takeaway containers, so Bryn checked out the kitchen's sole cupboard, a light maple cabinet that stood as tall as the fridge. She was slightly awed by the dishes she found: beautiful pottery plates, bowls and mugs in earthy blues, greens and russet. Then her eyes lit on another surprise, a bottle of red wine with a little note hanging around its neck: *Thank you for staying at River's Sigh B & B. Enjoy!*

The gift made her realize that she hadn't asked Jo how much the room cost per night. She decided it was probably best not to know. Treating herself would be an early Christmas present.

She set two places on the gorgeous eating plank, arranged the cold food prettily on a big platter she found, and put the dessert in the fridge.

Surveying her work, she had a moment of panic. Sean really was going to think she was some freaky, overly invested, "smothering mother" type.

"No one wants to be micromanaged, Bryn, so get it through your head and stop mothering everyone. I'm not one of your retards, and you don't have kids, remember? You *can't*."

Old words—Brad's—slammed into her head. She winced and closed her eyes for a moment. His ignorant use of the R-word had sent fury rippling through her at the time and still created waves of anger in her now.

He could be so intentionally cruel, so quick to devalue any person who wasn't his version of "normal." She recognized his shallowness for what it was now— and knew that most of the accusations and insults he'd lobbed came from his issues, not hers. All the same, she'd be lying if she said he hadn't deeply affected her. When would she be free of his nasty voice? *When?*

There is nothing weird or "motherly" about putting food out—or if there is, it's in a nice, good way, she assured herself. People who care about each other do nice things for each other—not that she cared about Sean, of course. That would be psycho.

She opened her eyes, thought of the wine, and made an executive decision. She poured two glasses, placed one by the dinner plate she'd intended for Sean, and took hers to the living room.

Take that, Brad, she thought. If I'm going to make some huge faux pas, I'll err on the side of looking like I'm shamelessly pursuing the poor accident victim, not trying to *mother* him.

Bryn flicked on a standing floor lamp behind the couch and located Steve. Wiped out by their adventures, he had claimed the only chair in the living room—a low slung recliner filled with cushions. His audible snoring made her smile as she sat down on the couch and curled her legs beneath her. Jo had been right about the couch. It was a tiny curved affair that even two people sitting together would find very cozy. It would be terrible for sleeping on.

A plush mink blanket lay across one of the couch arms. She ran her hand over its silky softness, but resisted wrapping herself in it. She wasn't cold and Sean might still be chilled and need it when he was finished in the bath. A well-stocked bookshelf filled one wall and caught her eye. She considered perusing the titles and reading for a bit, but decided she was too comfortable to move and just enjoyed her wine instead. It was velvety on her tongue and tasted of blackberries and plums, with something darker and richer underneath. Yum.

She was about to cave to the increasingly loud nagging of her stomach—and planned to top up her wine glass—when Sean emerged from the bathroom, rubbing his hair dry with a thick white towel. "Holy cow, it smells amazing out here."

He was barefoot and wearing gray sweatpants and a navy and white baseball shirt. Bryn found him—and the outfit—so ridiculously appealing that she was momentarily speechless.

Sean glanced toward the kitchen, then did a double take when he saw the arranged plates.

Bryn's cheeks flamed immediately. She shook her head. "Uh, I hope you don't mind or think I'm being some weird mother hen or something…" Shut up, Bryn, shut up, shut up, she told herself and managed to say something more normal. "It just all looked so good that I thought we should do it justice."

Sean looked back at her and his voice was soft, "Are you kidding me? It looks fantastic. I can't wait to dig in." He registered the glass in her hand. "There's wine?"

"I know. Crazy, right?"

He grinned.

Bryn's insides flip-flopped. She bit her lip and stood. "Well, shall we?"

"We shall." Sean ducked back into the bathroom and reappeared without the towel, but carrying his backpack. He unzipped it as he neared the table, then paused.

"What's wrong?"

"Nothing. Nothing at all." He laughed, pulled a bottle of spiced rum from his pack, set it near the wine, and pushed the backpack against the wall. "It's probably redundant with the wine, but you never know. I'd thought we might want to warm our bones."

"And speaking of that, how are your bones?" Bryn asked, then almost choked on the mouthful of wine she'd just taken.

"My bones... are good. Great, actually. That tub— you'll have to check it out. It's amazing. No jets, but so deep. Great for soaking in."

Bryn grabbed the food from the oven and filled their plates, then settled herself on one of the high-backed stools, hyper conscious of how close Sean was to her as he did the same.

He raised his wineglass. "To not freezing our asses off in cold vehicles in the middle of the night. This is much better, hey?"

She smiled and lifted her glass to his. "Hear, hear."

"And to new friends." His eyes burned into hers. "Who I assure you I don't see as 'mother hen-like' at all."

She sipped again and hoped it wasn't a gulp.

"I was thinking while I was in the tub," he added, "that crashing here like this, together, is kind of weird, hey? Sort of awkward."

She nodded. Wait for it, she thought, sure he was going to explain how he didn't want her to get the wrong idea.

"But it's also, well… super fun, isn't it?"

She smiled.

"And romantic—" Before she could respond to the word, Sean held up a hand. "Wait, sorry. Please don't worry. I didn't mean I think we're going to be romantic, like physically or anything. I meant it in the other definition of the word. Idyllic, picturesque, fairy tale like… Uh…" He shook his head helplessly.

Relief coursed through Bryn and she burst out laughing. She was weird, no doubt about it, but maybe, just maybe, he was the same kind of weird. "Don't worry. I know exactly what you mean."

And just like that, the easy flow they'd enjoyed as they adventured down the unfamiliar road, looking for River's Sigh, was back.

"Olive?" Bryn asked.

"You know it," Sean replied.

Chapter 7

SEAN STRETCHED BACK IN HIS chair, unable to eat another bite. The meal had been wonderful, the drinking companionable and cheering—but the conversation and the excellent company sitting so close to him even more so. Throughout the evening, he'd caught himself staring at Bryn a little too openly (Thanks, Captain Morgan!), but her eyes seemed to meet his just as often, so he didn't feel too self-conscious—just happy.

Bryn waved her hand, gesturing at the pillaged food, the empty wine bottle and her tumbler of rum. "I just want you to know, I don't do this all the time. This is not normal for me." Her voice was both earnest and conspiratorial.

"Well, since we're in confession mode. This is *totally* my normal." Sean winked, enjoying the cute pink flush that spread across her fair skin. Nothing made Gemma blush, and her face never gave away her emotions, happy, sad or otherwise, unless she wanted it to. Sean imagined it would be difficult for Bryn to hide her feelings—and he hoped she'd find it impossible to lie bald-faced, then wondered why it mattered to him.

"Yep, I do this all the time," he continued. "Put my truck off the road, convince my rescuer to shack up with me at a B & B, ply her with food and alcohol… it's so commonplace now, it's gotten boring."

"Really?"

Sean laughed and shook his head. "No, not really—not *ever* until now. I only had rum on me when I crashed because it's Christmas. It was supposed to be a gift for my buddy, the guy I'm staying with over the holidays. I don't normally carry bottles of booze around."

Bryn sipped her rum, deep enough into the bottle now that she no longer pulled a face at the hard alcohol's taste. "Okay, the booze is unusual, but what about the other stuff?"

"My truck? I swear that's the first accident I've ever been in."

"That's not what I—"

"River's Sigh?" He shook his head. "I promise, I've never been here before."

Bryn giggled and her cheeks went rosy. "I was actually trying to find out if you, to use your own words, 'shack up' often?" Her face burned even brighter.

"Ah," Sean said. "The truth?"

She nodded.

"Well, it's kind of a mood killer and might forever wreck your flattering vision of me as some Casanova or something, but no…"

Bryn leaned in.

"No women. No *woman*," Sean continued. "My long-term relationship ended six months ago and my ex took my heart with her. Not in a sweet, longing to be back together way." He took a big swig of rum. "More like in a maybe true love doesn't even exist sort of way. I always wanted to fall in love, get married, and grow old and decrepit with someone. But maybe that's not a thing anymore."

Bryn sucked in air, like she'd received a hard pinch.

Sean scowled as he considered his next words, then shook his head. "Gemma, my ex, never really wanted to be with me, or at least not exclusively, but I, like a total idiot, didn't see the truth. I was always sure she'd come around or that deep down she did feel the same, just didn't want to be vulnerable and admit it or something." He stopped talking abruptly, feeling every bit of the wine and rum he'd imbibed. The stuff was like truth serum. Bryn was going to think he was the biggest flake—

"Oh," she said, "*Oh*." The words were more breath than sound and seemed involuntary. They reminded Sean of sex and his gut tightened with arousal. "I know exactly how you feel," she said. "*Exactly*. When someone you love doesn't love you, never loved you... only ever loved the idea of some you that never existed, could never exist..." Her face scrunched and Sean worried she might cry, but she held onto her pain tightly, and her voice remained steady, her eyes dry.

"And you're the last one to discover it… It's the worst. It makes you feel like the biggest fool—like you can't trust your own instincts."

Bryn stopped talking and put her hand on Sean's knee as if unable to continue, but still desperate to communicate. Almost as fast as her hand touched down, however, she yanked it back. Sean knew why. He'd felt it too—an electric jolt that passed between them. Their eyes locked, and Bryn stood quickly, her fluid movements belying the amount of alcohol in her system. "We need to move into the living room for this," she announced.

What did she mean by "this"? Sean's fevered blood and alcohol fueled hormones clashed with his brain. On one hand he was hoping, so hoping, she was referring to something physical. On the other hand, he liked Bryn—liked in a way and to a degree that completely caught him by surprise. He didn't want to screw up the chance they might keep seeing each other after this night by… Screwing. He'd learned the hard way he wasn't a casual guy about anything really, let alone sex.

Instead of moving to the small couch or cozy chair, however, she stared at the dirty dishes and empty food containers. "I should clean this up."

"No way. You've done enough. I'll tackle the mess in the morning."

Bryn's eyes widened and she looked stricken. "Oh no. Have I been totally overbearing? I'm sorry."

Sean raised his eyebrow, confused.

"Have I done too much?"

"Not at all. This whole night has been lovely. *You* are lovely."

Bryn flushed yet again and Sean decided he had a new favorite color. At least on her. Pink. Totally.

She motioned toward the counter. "Are you sure? It wouldn't take me long."

"I'm sure." Sean took her hand and tugged her gently toward the couch—and tried to ignore the echoing tug of his insides at even this simple connection with her.

She settled cross-legged on the floor by the couch, despite his repeated encouragement to take it herself, and he fiddled with the small gas fireplace. Soon a cozy glow filled the small room. He collected the rum bottle, then motioned at her empty glass in silent question.

"Sooo much rum," Bryn groaned—then grinned. "But yes, please, sure."

It was just after midnight and Sean was feeling the long day, but he didn't want the evening to end. He topped up his drink too, then settled on one end of the couch, so he could watch Bryn's face as they talked.

"So now you know my life story," he said.

"Hardly."

"Okay, well, you know I'm jaded and angry. What's your sad tale? Who's this idiot who loved some version of you that you aren't, instead of the great person you are?"

Bryn focused her gaze on the fireplace's small orange flame. "Oh yeah, I'm really great."

"You're right," Sean amended. "'Great' doesn't cut it."

She nodded like he was being serious, not joking. Her resigned acceptance of some ridiculously low opinion of herself killed him. It was just as bizarre as her weird insecurity whenever she did something nice for him—like she expected him to bite her head off for setting out dinner or for asking if he was all right. Whoever Bryn's ex was, he must've been a piece of work.

"Yep," he repeated with emphasis. "Great doesn't cut it at all. Brave. Generous. Kind. Gorgeous. Any one of those is much better."

"Yeah, right," she said, but her smile returned, curving her luscious mouth, a mouth that he'd like to—

"The booze has obviously gone straight to your head," she continued. "You're drunk."

"Oh yeah, I am," he agreed happily because what else could he say? She was right, but it wasn't just the booze. It was her.

"Now tell me," he prodded gently, "who's this guy who hurt you so badly and stole all your confidence?"

Bryn sipped her drink, then stretched. "He is... no one. Or no one I want to talk about right now. Why ruin such a great night?"

"I'll drink to that." Sean stretched his glass toward her and she clinked hers gently against his.

"Earlier you mentioned you're an event planner, but then we veered away to some other topic. Tell me about your job. How'd you get into it? Do you love it? What does it entail?"

Sean smiled at the barrage of questions. "How I got into it... I got roped into planning a birthday party for my sister Marnie's daughter and it kind of snowballed from there. I enjoyed it so much I left a marketing job I was good at, but that didn't bring me a lot of satisfaction."

Bryn nodded as if that made perfect sense, not like she thought he was nuts, which was some people's response. Sean found himself sharing details he usually didn't, like how the big birthday had taken place five months after Marnie's breast cancer diagnosis and the simultaneous bailing of her husband and how desperately Sean had wanted to cheer up and encourage the whole family.

"Fighting cancer and raising two kids alone was a struggle to say the least," he continued, "but Marnie managed. She's ten years' cancer free now and unflaggingly cheerful and optimistic—but still single and adamant that she's going to stay that way. I still try to give her a lot of support, and I'm close to my niece and nephew who are both in high school now."

"You're a pretty nice brother."

Sean shrugged off the compliment. "I was a shit

when we were kids. I'm just trying to even things up."

"And what do you like about it? Your job, I mean."

He cleared his throat. "Okay, what I love… Meeting different people and helping them celebrate their lives' most special moments—and helping them bring their dream settings and decorations into reality. What I like least… Sometimes people forget that at the end of the day, the actual event being celebrated—the marriage, the anniversary, the birthday—is the thing to focus on and really enjoy. People can get so fixated on tiny details, wanting everything just right, or wanting something they've always envisioned instead of paying attention to what the person at the heart of the event might prefer—and I get stressed out if I sense people are moving beyond what they can, or should, comfortably afford."

Bryn leaned back against the couch, rested her cheek on the seat cushion, and looked up at him. "You're so nice. If I ever have something big to celebrate, I want you to plan it. Promise you will." Her voice was soft and sleepy, the long day, the filling meal, the drinks obviously doing their work.

"You bet I will," he replied.

Bryn's head jerked as if she'd nodded off then re-awoke. She giggled. "Whoa, I'm sorry. You're losing me. I don't want to, but I'd better turn in."

"Sounds like a plan. Tomorrow will be another full day."

"Can we eat breakfast together before we say

good-bye?"

The question stabbed Sean. *Before we say good-bye.* Why would the words hurt when they hadn't even known each other for twenty-four hours? "I'd love that," Sean said. In his head he added, "for the rest of my life"—and knew he was a drunk fool. He helped Bryn up from the floor. She glided off to the bathroom, just the tiniest bit wobbly on her feet, then headed into the bedroom. A light clicked on and shone through a crack at the bottom of the door.

Sean heard the smallest "Oh" of appreciation, then the sound of her falling into bed in the other room made him smile. The light clicked off after a minute or so and Sean pulled off his sweats so he was just in his boxers and T-shirt and stretched out on the couch. Or, rather, he tried to stretch out. After a few tosses and turns, he changed strategies and settled himself on the carpet in front of the fireplace instead, using one of the throw cushions as a pillow and the blanket from the couch as bedding. It was pretty comfortable and after a few minutes he even had company. Steve moved from the chair and curled up behind his knees.

Sean was drowsily reliving the events of the past eight hours, marveling at how his misfortune (a.k.a. his stupidity) with the truck had turned into the best luck he'd ever enjoyed, when the bedroom door opened. Then Bryn softly called, "Sean? Are you still awake?"

Chapter 8

SEAN STOOD ON THE OTHER side of the bed from Bryn. He had gone as far as turning his corner of the blankets down, but then he stopped and looked at her. The light from the small bedside lamp made him look angelic— or temptingly devilish, she wasn't sure which.

"Are you positive?" he asked.

She nodded, although admittedly she hadn't realized he'd stripped down to his boxers and T-shirt when she asked. She was wearing a long tank top and panties, of course, but her legs were bare too. The idea of him almost naked in bed beside her…

"Totally," she said, embarrassed by how raw and croaky her voice was. He could probably tell how attractive she found him. After all, she practically swooned every time he looked at her, said the kindest word, and now… This.

"I promise I won't take advantage," he'd said when she first offered to share the bed, an assurance she both appreciated and found slightly disappointing.

They each sat down on their separate sides, and Bryn reached over and clicked out the light. Velvet darkness blanketed the room and for a moment they were both completely still. Then the mattress dipped and shuddered. Sean had lain down and was arranging himself for sleep. She followed his lead and eased onto her side, facing into the center of the bed. Was Sean a side or stomach or back sleeper? And if the former, was he facing toward her or away?

The few minutes she'd been in bed by herself before deciding it wasn't fair for her to get the good mattress while he froze on the floor hadn't been enough to warm the sheets. She rubbed her legs up and down the soft cotton, trying to heat them. Even that simple movement felt intensely erotic.

Beside her, Sean sighed deeply—and she realized he was indeed facing her. She shivered a little.

"Cold?" he whispered.

"Not too bad. The bed will warm up soon."

"Yeah." Sean sighed again, sounding very content. "I love this duvet. It's like resting under a marshmallow."

Under the cover of darkness, and with the added courage from the evening's earlier drinking, Bryn decided to speak her mind, knowing if she didn't do so now, she'd probably chicken out in the morning. "Maybe it's weird to say this since we only met because of your accident, but I had a really nice time tonight. I'm glad we met."

Sean didn't reply immediately, but the mattress shifted again. In the shadows, now that Bryn's eyes had adjusted to the dark, she saw Sean prop himself up on one elbow and study her. "I'm glad too," he said softly. "It was a great night. In fact, there's only one thing that would make it even better."

Bryn laughed a bit nervously. "Oh, yeah? What's that?"

"Before you went to bed I wanted to kiss you good night."

"You did?"

"Yes. Very much."

Something thrilled deep inside Bryn. Sean liked her, was attracted to her. It wasn't all one-sided or imagined.

"Well, it's not too late for *one* kiss."

"It's not?"

"No."

"I don't want some chaste, gentle lip brush thing," he warned.

"Oh no?"

"No, I want to give you the kind of kiss you really feel—in all your parts."

"Oh, really?" She tried hard to sound skeptical, not as breathless as the idea—*all your parts*—made her.

Instead of answering with words, Sean responded with action. He remained propped on one elbow, taking her in with his eyes, and reached toward her with his free hand. He stroked her hair, then ran his fingers along the side of her face, pausing at the crease of her eye, the peak of her cheekbone, the corner of her mouth… He hadn't even kissed her yet, but good grief, she was already feeling a lot of things in *a lot* of her parts—things she'd worried she might never feel again.

He smoothed his hand down her shoulder and arm, stopping at her wrist, which he encircled with his fingers. Then he brought her hand to his mouth and kissed the tender place over her radial artery on the inside of her wrist. Her heart thumped so wildly she was sure he could feel it against his lips.

When he pushed gently on her shoulder, she fell to rest on her back beneath him. He pressed a kiss to her jaw just below her ear and then another to her neck. One of his hands moved between her and the mattress and the other traced her ribs and hip. Then both hands found the curve of her butt and pulled her close.

Bryn was breathing hard now, and she inhaled sharply as she felt his muscular legs twine with hers and his pelvis lightly grind against her, his erection pressing the softness of her belly. A wave of pleasure crashed through her. "Oh…" she moaned, but the sound was quelled by his mouth.

For a few minutes, Bryn lost all conscious thought, was aware only of a flood of sensation. Sean's lips, soft and gentle on hers. The stubble on his chin, seductively rough against her skin. His scent—faint eucalyptus from his soak, the tiniest hint of musk breaking through the mask of fresh, masculine deodorant, sweet undertones of rum… Why did the combination make her stomach tighten with desire? His mouth firmer on hers, insistent. Her opening to the press of him—

He teased her tongue with his own, then searched, then demanded an equally intense response.

His hands on the small of her back kneaded in rhythm with his tongue and Bryn was conscious of the liquid heat pooling between her legs and a feral urge low in her center. Then Sean moved suddenly, shifting his attention lower, kissing and licking the sensitive arch of her exposed throat. She couldn't keep from groaning.

When he found the hollow of her neck with his tongue, then gently sucked, she yelped. Sean seemed undone by the noise and collapsed, panting, beside her.

"Okay then, that's out of the way. Good night," he said finally.

It was a moment before Bryn could respond, but then she laughed, her own breathing a little ragged.

"No, seriously," he added. "You are… That was…" Seemingly at a loss for words, he didn't complete either thought. Instead he nudged her onto her side, facing her away from himself, and curved his body around hers. "Is this okay?"

"Yeah," Bryn agreed happily.

For a few seconds they were completely silent, then Sean added, "Did you like that as much I did?"

"Couldn't you tell?" Bryn asked.

"Hell yeah, I could."

Bryn giggled softly, too sleepy and happy to bother feeling embarrassed. She'd leave all self-doubt and self-berating until the morning when they said good-bye. A tide of wistfulness swept over her. She hadn't even known Sean for twenty-four hours, but she was going to miss him. A lot. Was it remotely possible that they could continue to see each other? Maybe arrange to meet for a date in the new year and see if they still liked each other, if maybe they had something?

Sean's arm on her waist grew heavier and his breathing slowed; he was obviously falling asleep. Bryn sighed and curled into him, letting herself fully enjoy the moment. Why couldn't she pretend they had a chance? Who was to say they didn't? Maybe he didn't want kids, not everyone did.

Sean stirred and hugged Bryn closer, then mumbled sleepily, "I think I want to marry you."

What the hell? Bryn's brain bolted awake, all sweet dregs of sleepy, sexy feelings momentarily obliterated. What kind of weirdo talks about marriage after one kiss? Then Sean let out a soft, boozy exhale and Bryn relaxed. It was the alcohol talking, removing all inhibitions. Hadn't she just been fantasizing about some possible future too? If her thoughts had been spoken aloud because inebriation turned off her internal self-censor, she would've looked equally out to lunch.

Sean exhaled again, but it wasn't his warm breath on her skin that made Bryn shiver and want to resume their long, sweet kiss and move onto all sorts of other things. No—since she was fully admitting her own lack of sobriety and her raging attraction to Sean—she let herself privately acknowledge something else. His words had filled her with a longing that went deeper than desire for physical pleasure—though heaven help her, she was pining for that in spades too.

What if marriage, not to Sean most likely, obviously, but to someone, sometime, wasn't really permanently off the table?

"You're drunk," she said as much to herself as to him.

"Oh yeah, I am," he murmured, a smile in his voice. "On happiness."

The teasing echo of their earlier exchange made Bryn's stomach flip with something she didn't want to admit was joy, but couldn't help feeling anyway. They already had an inside joke.

"Yep," he continued in a dreamy rumble. "I'll build us a cabin like this somewhere. We can hole up, make love whenever we want, raise a bunch of babies—"

This time, Bryn's whole body stiffened and she pulled away. Drunken blather or not, of course a man as great as Sean would want the whole package, not a damaged—

She didn't get very far. Sean clasped her hip, keeping her close. "Hey, hey," he soothed. "It's okay. Are you having a bad dream?"

Bryn was touched—and surprised—that even in the haze between sleeping and wakefulness, Sean was so tuned into her feelings. Her problem, however, was the opposite of what he suggested. She had let herself have a *happy* dream. If only her playing pretend could've lasted till morning.

"Goodnight, lovely Bryn. Sweet dreams." Sean pressed his lips to her shoulder in one last lingering kiss. Bryn waffled, then made a decision. She let her body soften and form to his again. She would allow herself this one night, this temporary but oh-so-sweet delusion.

Chapter 9

BRYN STUDIED HER FACE IN the small bathroom mirror
and wished she had left the cabin before Sean woke up.
She had managed—very regretfully, wanting to stay
cozied up with him for the rest of the morning—to slip
out of his embrace and exit the bed without waking
him, but now she heard him rustling about in the
kitchen.

What had she been thinking the night before? Answer: nothing smart. Plus, she looked as hungover as
she felt, which made her extra plain and limp seeming.
She was, as Brad used to say, blah and bland in the
extreme.

Worse than her pounding head and unkind self-
talk, however, was the crash and burn of the lovely
fantasy she'd been indulging, regarding sweet, sexy
Sean. Yes, she'd managed to enjoy her delicious
daydream through the night, even after the ice water
dose of reality his "raise a bunch of babies" line had
thrown at her. But it was morning now. The fun of her
late-night waking dream was over.

She scrubbed her pale as milk face hard with a

washcloth, hoping to wake herself up and possibly get a bit of color in her cheeks. Then she forced herself to get a grip. If she didn't leave the washroom soon, it would seem like she had some horribly embarrassing problem. Sean would be scared to go in. How humiliating!

Steve was apparently frustrated by what a ninny she was too. He positioned himself on the other side of the bathroom door and commenced a low panting whine. She finally crept out as quietly as she could, but it was no use. Steve gamboled about in ecstasy at her reappearance, and Sean turned from the sink of dishes he was washing, his scruffy face lit with a big smile. Good grief, the man could almost freeze to death, eat his body weight in heavy food, drink half a 26er of rum and still wake up looking super hot and ready for anything. If she didn't like him so much, she'd have to hate him. He probably didn't even get morning breath. Bryn was suddenly beyond relieved that she'd snuck into the bathroom first. At least her teeth were brushed and she was clean.

"Good morning," he said cheerily.

"Yeah," she mumbled, then cringed at her tone. She wasn't grouchy—just confused. Sean still sounded friendly, like he still *liked* her... but that wasn't possible and she wasn't going to pretend to herself that it was.

His smile didn't falter, but he spoke a little quieter. "Can I make you coffee before we go for breakfast?"

Right. Breakfast. Her uninhibited rum-soaked question before she'd gone to bed, before they shared that kiss, came back to her. *Can we eat breakfast together before we say good-bye?* Ugh. Had she sounded like she was begging, pleading, being desperate? Probably.

He'd most likely only said yes to be kind—and she didn't want him to feel obligated now, just because they'd kissed and she probably had "I'm a dork and have already fallen for you" written all over her forehead.

But it *wasn't* a casual kiss, her brain argued. Or it sure didn't feel like one to her anyway—but that was the problem. Lots of people shared kisses, and a whole lot more, as easily as saying Cheers! She wasn't going to repeat her old mistakes and read a bunch into it. The day Brad told her it was over, that he wanted someone "whole" who could have a family, she'd been utterly stunned. And twisting the knife of shock was the fact they'd made love the night before—no, scratch that. She now knew it had nothing to do with love. They'd had sex, but wild, really good sex. When she asked Brad how, why that had even been possible, she'd been permanently changed and shaken by his terse reply and the meanness in his eyes.

"Grow up, Bryn."

Even now, recalling the memory, she wilted in humiliation and hurt. Everything she thought was special, was sacred was… nothing. And she had grown up since then. She saw a lot of things more clearly, much more clearly—but she missed her old self, the trusting, fun-loving, easily sensual person she'd been—the woman who had come out to play just a little bit with Sean the night before.

Sean. Bryn crashed back to the present in a hurry. She'd almost forgotten he was right there, that he'd asked her a question. He was staring. She flushed.

"Coffee?" he repeated softly.

She shook her head abruptly. "No thanks. I've got calls to make. I'll leave my stuff here for now and come back for it."

Sean hesitated, a serving spatula he'd been drying in one hand, a black and cream striped tea towel in the other. He set both items down on the counter and nodded slowly. "Oh... okay. Should I just meet you in the dining hall then? How long do you need for the phone? Fifteen minutes, half an hour?"

Why didn't he understand he didn't have to keep being so nice? "Not long, but you don't have to meet me. It's fine."

"But I thought we were going to..." Sean trailed off and resumed drying dishes. When he spoke again, his voice was matter-of-fact and much less buoyant. "It's going to be a busy day. We'll need to eat. I'll see you there."

Bryn shrugged, slid her boots on, grabbed her jacket, and sprinted from the cabin.

She finished zipping her coat as she tramped along

the trail, dry snow squeaking under her boots. Although it was already nine in the morning, the sun was just beginning its slow rise and the sky beyond the snow-draped evergreens was pink and purple. Bryn couldn't fully appreciate the beauty, however. She kept remembering Sean's change in demeanor and realized—baffling and impossible as it seemed—that maybe she'd confused *him*, had hurt his feelings even. But how would that make sense? Still, she knew the difference between a wounded ego and its angry kind of "sad" (Brad!) and genuine disappointment. Had Sean really felt the latter when she hadn't been enthusiastic about breakfast?

No. She shook her head at herself, impatient with her undying skill for self-deception and wishful thinking. His mood change probably came from pondering the chores of the upcoming day. And his tender whisperings while they cuddled that kept sneaking back to torture her? They were the drunken ramblings of a sweet man who'd had a good night and who thought the person he was whispering to was asleep. Besides, even if there had been an iota of sincerity in them—a big *if*—his fantasy involved kids, so that was the end, kaput.

As Bryn neared the big circular parking lot, a family of five emerged from the dining hall, laughing and jostling each other. Bryn pulled out her cellphone to distract herself from her sad, lame thoughts and to keep herself from tearing up. There was so much beauty around her—beauty that she was always a witness to, never a part of.

Powering her phone on, Jo's claim regarding cell service proved true. Bryn had only enough signal to show she had seven voicemails—all from her mother's number—but not enough to check the actual messages.

Chapter 10

THE SCENT OF FRESH CINNAMON buns and coffee flirted with Sean before he even reached the dining hall. Normally tracking down the source of the delicious smell and eating his fill would be a priority, but today it was almost an unwelcome distraction. He didn't want breakfast—or he did, but only if he could get things sorted out with Bryn. What had changed? Why could she hardly look at him? The evening before, her blush had been cute and endearing. Today it was painful, obviously caused by discomfort, not mutual attraction.

You know exactly what changed, you idiot, the nastier side of his inner voice said. And he did. The knowledge had fallen into his head, thudding like snow sliding off a roof, as he followed Bryn's footsteps along the path toward the dining hall.

The night had unfolded like some perfect dream, and even before that crazy, mind-blowing kiss, Sean had known one thing with his whole being: he was *interested*-interested in Bryn. It wasn't just a physical attraction. He really wanted to get to know her—had thought that maybe they had something, or, even crazier, that maybe love at first sight, or close to it, was actually a thing.

Yeah, because in addition to being an idiot, he was a psycho—

Except he really wasn't, though he couldn't fault Bryn if that's what she thought. He was something much worse—a romantic. You'd have thought being involved with Gemma for so long would've cured him, but no...

He reached the stairs leading to the dining hall's porch, but procrastinated about entering. What if she ignored him, or worse, told him in no uncertain terms to get lost? He took his time kicking the snow off his boots and thoroughly brushing it from his backpack, which he'd repacked and brought with him in case Bryn wasn't comfortable with him returning to the cabin with her. Everything had been going so well, had been so sweet... and then he'd had to mutter that stupid crap about thinking he wanted to marry her.

The feelings were sincere, and not because of the alcohol. He'd found himself playing the What If game all night. What if their accidental meeting, their one night, turned into something more? What if they really did become a couple? What if they got along as well as they seemed to... for life? What if he got to satisfy the desire he had for her, in every way, in all sorts of ways, all the time? What if, what if, what if?

Expressing the wish that those What Ifs triggered,

however? Whispering it aloud, regardless of whether he'd thought she was asleep or not? That stupidity was totally the rum's fault. Of course, he should've kept his premature hope to himself. Of course, being that intense would make him seem like a mental case. And of course, she'd be put off by a guy who'd say such things after one great night and one great kiss—though seriously the word "great" did not begin to cover it for him.

He knew he'd felt Bryn tense and try to slide away. He, like a goof, had thought she was having a bad dream. Now he knew it was because she'd thought she'd accidentally ended up with a desperate could-be psycho.

He needed to figure out the best way to redeem himself, if that was even possible. Should he just come out and directly apologize for how he must've seemed? Admit he'd crossed a line?

Should he beg her to give him another chance, to see him even just once more to see if they might have something? (Oh yeah, that sounded smart—because begging worked so well in relationships.)

Maybe a better plan would be to ignore his fears about what was bothering her, plunk himself down for breakfast and then casually ask if she wanted to do coffee or something over the holidays—only if it worked easily for her, of course. No stress. No biggie. (Right. Because he pulled off *casual* so casually.)

A smiling older couple in red toques and matching

scarves approached, said hello, then climbed the stairs. "Are you coming in too?" the gentleman asked, holding the door open.

Sean guessed he couldn't stall much longer. "Yes, thanks," he said. He was scanning the room for Bryn even before the heavy oak door shut behind him.

He spotted her almost immediately, though she was well away from the massive communal table. She stood, back to the room, bowed over the phone. He couldn't hear what she was saying, but her body language made his jaw tense. Something was wrong.

Jo appeared at his elbow, carrying a platter stacked high with pancakes. "Good morning! I hope you slept comfortably after your harrowing evening."

If only she knew *how* comfortably. "Wonderfully, thanks."

Jo nodded but her gaze followed his toward Bryn. For a second, she looked mildly quizzical, but then she smiled. "There's a coffee trolley near Bryn, or, if you hang tight for a second, I can fetch you a cup. Just seat yourself whenever you're ready and dig in."

"Thanks, Jo." He glanced toward the coffee trolley, half a foot from where Bryn stood. Well, better now than never—and he was a coffee guy, always desperate for his first hit of the day.

Sean was careful not to crowd Bryn, who acknowledged his approach with a small nod before she refocused on her phone call, one arm crossed over her stomach like she was clutching it. He filled a large mug with coffee, then added a generous serving of cream.

"But Mom—" Bryn said, suddenly loud. She glanced over at the rest of the dining hall's guests and lowered her voice. Sean tried not to feel like it was a good sign that she didn't seem to mind if he overheard her. "*Mom*," she repeated. "We've had these Christmas plans for six months. I took two weeks off work. It's not fair to change them on a whim."

She was quiet a moment, listening, then said, "It is so a big deal. To me."

More silence on Bryn's side—and a buzzing of chatter from her mother that Sean didn't quite catch. He caught Bryn's eye and noticed she was coffee free. He motioned at his mug and mouthed, "Want some?"

She bit her bottom lip so hard, white idents from her teeth showed. Then she nodded. He filled her a mug, then held up cream. Got another nod. He added a dollop, then held up sugar. She shook her head.

He placed her doctored cup within her reach on the trolley, then went to find two empty chairs at the table, hoping she'd join him.

As he walked away, he heard her speak again in a low, pain-filled voice, "But what about me? It's five sleeps until Christmas. I drove all day yesterday. I'm only three hours away…"

Another pause, then a sad sounding, "Yes, I know Christmas is more fun spent with little kids, but no, sorry, I can't make it work this time… I just can't."

Whatever did or didn't get said next was lost on Sean, and while he hadn't meant to invade Bryn's privacy and she hadn't seemed to be offended by his presence, he felt badly for overhearing her private family matters all the same. He sat down a good distance away from the other guests—the older couple who had entered with him, a mother with two teenage boys, and three middle-aged women who were laughing about how they stayed at River's Sigh B & B so often they should be on the payroll.

"I wish we weren't checking out today," one of them added. "I'd like to stay here forever." She dragged out the word "forever" like a kid would and Sean smiled, relating to how she felt.

He'd just helped himself to a cinnamon bun and said yes to Jo's offer to do him up some bacon and eggs when Bryn appeared at his side, coffee in hand.

"Um," she said, sounding apologetic. Instantly, Sean knew she wasn't going to sit down. The spark of hope kindled by her approach fizzled into disappointment.

"Thanks for the coffee."

"No problem."

"But about breakfast... I'm really sorry. It doesn't work. I've got to... well, sort some stuff out."

Nailed it, Sean thought, noting that even just twelve hours ago she would've shared the details, not said "stuff." Last night had obviously been a one off. She'd only relaxed with him so fully, let her guard down so totally, because she thought she'd never see him again.

He stood up, wanting to kiss her once more, but settled for extending his hand. "It was really nice to meet you, Bryn. I meant—" He was about to say that he'd meant everything he said the previous night, but remembered his stupid marriage comment just in time. "Have a good Christmas, okay?"

Was it his imagination or did a fleeting look of disappointment flash in her eyes? Probably wishful thinking. She took his hand, hesitated just a moment, then shook it firmly.

"I…" She paused as if reconsidering whatever she'd been about to say, then simply said, "You have a good Christmas too. Good-bye, Sean."

He tried and failed not to follow her with his eyes all the way back to the office doorway, where she spoke with Jo and Callum for a few minutes. Then she left the hall and headed into the wintery day.

Sean's pity party at the final-seeming farewell was cut short when Callum arrived with the crispy bacon and sunny-side up eggs Jo had promised and news that the snow plow had been by. The highway was finally passable. It was his next words, however, that really pricked Sean's interest.

"I volunteered to grab Bryn's car for her since she's decided to stay on for a bit. I'll walk you to your truck if you want."

So that was that. It really was bye-bye, Bryn. Sean

tried to feel the gratitude he had the previous evening. He'd met a great person and had a great night—one that he'd remember forever. He should be happy, not dismal. The pep talk didn't work.

Chapter 11

"THAT SHOULD BE THE LAST of it," Callum said, putting a large basket of Christmas baking on the counter in Trout cabin. "Are you sure you're only staying a week? You look like you're moving in permanently."

Bryn forced a smile she didn't feel, thinking about all the goodies and gifts stored in the suitcases and boxes that surrounded her. "There was a change of plans. It was supposed to be a big family do, so I had a little something for everyone."

Callum grimaced. "I'm sorry. I didn't mean to poke a bruise."

"No apologies necessary. Thank you so much for grabbing my car and helping me haul all this stuff in here."

"No problem." Callum pulled a square of ivory cardstock from his jacket pocket and handed it to Bryn. Curling ivy, holly and bells in soft shades of green, gold and crimson framed a schedule of events written in beautiful black cursive. "Jo and I usually go for a holiday this time of year, but we decided we wanted to have Christmas at home for once. I think we got a bit carried away, but it should be fun. Please join in for any or all of the festivities."

"The more the merrier?"

"Absolutely—and every event's dog friendly, so feel free to bring Steve."

Steve bounced around as if to say he heard the invitation and Bryn had better not forget it.

"He does think he's the life of the party," she said. Steve bounced higher and Callum chuckled. She thanked him again and moments later found herself alone once more.

Despite all the suitcases, bags and boxes cluttering the place, the cabin felt a little lonely. Nope, she would not go there. Yes, it had been extra cozy last night, but she would enjoy being on her own here just fine. She scanned the activities, thought they all looked like they'd be more fun with a partner, and shook her head at herself.

"You're hopeless," she scolded aloud, then propped the schedule beside the coffee maker and got busy. Soon a pile of shiny wrapped presents stood in one corner of the living room, a small stack of games decorated the coffee table, and the fridge and counter were bursting with tins of baked goods and homemade chocolates.

She remembered spying a large glass bowl in the cabin's tall cupboard and dug it out. Inspired, she ran outside coatless and returned minutes later with sprigs of greenery she didn't think the nearby trees would miss. She filled the bowl with vintage metal ornaments she had purchased for each of her sisters and nieces. Someone might as well get to enjoy them, right? She tucked bits of pine here and there, then added strands of curling ribbon. Stepping back, she admired her work. The result was eye-catching and fun and looked especially spectacular juxtaposed with the cabin's stone and wood decor.

Next, Bryn rolled her suitcase into the bedroom and paused by the unmade bed. Wanting to kick herself for being so lame, but unable to resist, she lay down and rolled onto the side of the mattress Sean had slept on. She buried her face in the pillow his head had graced. Could she smell the faintest trace of him, or was she looney?

Knowing the answer to that, she climbed off the bed slowly and put her clothes away in the dresser, hung her one dress, then stashed her now empty suitcase and overnight bag in the closet.

Back in the kitchen, Bryn filched a chocolate covered cherry, her personal favorite and that of most of her nieces and nephews as well. She popped it into her mouth, then tossed a liver treat to eagerly awaiting Steve—at least one of them was feeling genuinely festive—and surveyed her work. It really was like she'd moved in.

Yes, things could've been worse, she thought, savoring the rich sweetness on her tongue. She could've gotten all the way to her parents' house to find a note on the door: We've ditched you for a last-minute Christmas down south with Clara's family.

At least staying here at River's Sigh, Bryn didn't feel hard done by. In fact, it was the reverse. It felt like she was giving herself the biggest Christmas present of her life. Plus, Jo had mentioned she and Callum were hosting a big Christmas dinner and had invited her. She wouldn't even have to eat alone.

The bowl of ornaments twinkled in the light from the window. She looked over at the wrapped presents once more too. Everything was pretty, but she was missing something vital. She searched all the drawers and cabinets, but had no luck. She started the coffee maker so she'd have something to warm her up when she returned, then pulled her outdoor clothes on, sure that Callum and Jo would help her out.

Bryn opened the door, stepped onto the porch—and shrieked at the top of her lungs.

Hand on her heart, she took a deep breath. "Sorry. Sorry. You scared me half to death."

For what it was worth, Sean looked equally startled. His arm was elevated, his hand frozen in an about-to-knock position. He lowered it and jammed his fists into his jeans' pockets. Bryn noticed a large rolling duffel bag at his feet, in addition to the backpack that she recognized from last night. What on earth?

"I was on my way to find a pine branch or something to use for a makeshift Christmas tree," Bryn blurted, then wanted to kick herself. Why would he care?

"Oh, yeah? Nice."

She nodded and they both stood there awkwardly. Why was he here again? He should be in town having his truck fixed by now, or be at his friend's house already.

"So... what's up?"

Sean just nodded. Then he suddenly straightened and squared his shoulders. "I, uh, just wanted to let you know I've had a change of plans too. After waiting for a tow for three hours, then getting my truck hooked up and dragged into a garage in Greenridge, which took another hour, I finally got to talk to a mechanic—and they don't have the part I need. Apparently, a massive tree stump kept me from going off into the river—and snapped my drive shaft. They can't get another one in until after Christmas. There's a used one at the wreckers, but if I have to shell out money for repairs, I'd rather go with parts that will have warranty."

Bryn nodded, unsure of how any of this pertained to her or explained why he was on her doorstep—not that she minded that he was, but she didn't want to get her hopes up either.

"So then I called the buddy I was going to be staying with and it turns out his mom had a bad fall."

"Oh no! Is she all right?"

Sean nodded. "She'll be okay, but understandably he wants to fly out to be with her—normally, his family does Christmas in July when the travel is better for everyone. And my sister, her kids and my mom are already headed for their all-inclusive in Mexico, which I declined to take part in, so..."

"So you're here?"

He nodded and she wondered feverishly what he thought her use of "here" meant. Was he expecting, *asking,* to stay with her again? Although part of her salivated at the idea, the sane—sober!—part of herself said no, no, *no.* It would be like voluntarily ripping her heart out of her chest and throwing it on the floor for him to stomp on.

Sean said something else, but lost in her own obsessive thoughts, Bryn only caught the last bit, "so it wouldn't be weird."

"Sorry, what?"

His brow furrowed.

She bit her lip. "I didn't hear you."

"Oh, I just said that I ended up renting a car and arranging to stay here at River's Sigh over the holidays. I'll be in a cabin called Rainbow. I wanted to give you the heads up, so if we ran into each other, it wouldn't be weird."

He shifted his weight foot to foot, then cleared his throat. Bryn didn't understand why he looked so uncomfortable. Maybe he was trying to say, without so many words, that he'd be around but didn't want her to get the wrong idea or to take it as a sign of him being interested or something?

"Look, Sean," she said, aiming to sound cool and collected—then noticed her stupid hands were shaking. "I know last night was… nothing. I don't have any expectations about seeing each other or anything, and I won't hold you to your marriage proposal. Relax." She meant the latter as a joke and hoped it came out lightly, not pathetically.

His eyebrow popped up and he scrubbed his stubble-rough chin. "So you *did* hear all that?"

She nodded and felt her cheeks burn despite the chilly air.

"But you thought I was the one who regretted the evening?"

"Yes, no… I don't know—but either way, it doesn't matter. It—us—wouldn't work." She noticed their breath was making little white clouds.

Sean looked flummoxed. "Why not?" Before she could answer, he added, "So you would be interested in seeing me if I was interested in seeing you?"

Yes! cheered part of Bryn. You can't, whispered another part. He's still young and he values family, *children*. He deserves the whole package, not some half woman. Bryn pressed her fists to her eyes, knowing she was probably smearing mascara all over her face, but not caring.

"What time will your cabin be ready?" she finally asked.

Sean studied her, looking concerned. "Jo said three o'clock-ish—so in an hour or so."

"We should talk inside then. It's freezing out here." Resigned, she stepped back and opened the door a crack. Now she wouldn't even get to remember the past night as one perfect little gem because it would always be linked to the scene about to unfold, the one where she disclosed her infertility and he, understandably, said she was right, that they wouldn't work long term. Ciao, Bryn.

Chapter 12

THE CABIN WAS TOASTY WARM and smelled deliciously of freshly cut pine and brewed coffee. Sean glanced around, unable to believe the changes in the cabin from the last time he'd seen it, just that morning. It was still gorgeous and cozy, but it looked… lived in, cared for, appreciated—and by some sweet homemaking goddess with great taste.

Bryn, though obviously just stashing stuff she'd planned to take to her family, had wrapped and stacked things in a way that would've suited any glossy magazine's "Home for Christmas" spread. He agreed she needed a tree though. Maybe when she got whatever was bugging her off her chest, she'd let him help get one.

As she peeled off her coat and boots, he tried to express his admiration of her talent. "You're an amazing homemaker, so how come you don't have a family of your own by now? Didn't you want one?"

He would've given his left hand to take the words back when he saw the expression that crossed her face. Then she laughed bitterly—the first such note he'd ever heard from her mouth—and changed his mind. He would've given both hands.

"Ironically, that's what I need to tell you, what will explain why seeing each other is a waste of time."

Without asking if he wanted one, she poured them each a coffee and fixed his how he liked it. She must've been paying him more attention earlier that morning than he thought.

She held her mug in a tight two-handed grip, but didn't take a sip. Instead she explained her failed marriage and what she blamed for its demise: herself, her inability to conceive and carry a child.

Sean had taken a throat-scalding gulp of coffee when she first started talking, but now, though his beverage had cooled to a drinkable temperature, he couldn't swallow a mouthful. He set the mostly untouched drink down on the coffee table and began to pace.

He recalled how Bryn shifted away from him in the night and understood that his words had been as terrible a blunder as he feared—but it wasn't his jest about marrying her that put her off. It was his thought-less line about having a bunch of babies. He had inadvertently hurt her.

As he tried to think of the best way to apologize, he wondered how stupidly often people were hurt by other people's casual comments and assumptions. Back when his sister had been undergoing treatment, he'd been enraged by people's ignorance. How people who didn't know Marnie had cancer would "compliment" her for losing so much weight and getting "so skinny." There they were raving about how great she looked, when she wasn't sure she was going to survive. One especially imbecilic woman had even said, "I'm sooo jealous."

When Marnie, tired of bizarre weight-obsessed comments from people she barely knew, explained she wasn't trying to size down, that she was sick, she had cancer, more than one person, instead of being embarrassed or apologetic, came back with some stupid line like, "Oh, well, you look great. I'm sure you're going to win the fight."

It had seemed almost unforgivable to him at the time—to be so obtuse and careless, so presumptuous that they knew someone else's story that they didn't even think before making such highly personal comments—and here he'd done the same rotten thing.

Bryn misunderstood his silence and put her mug down beside his. "Don't feel bad. It's okay. I knew it would change things."

"No, you don't get it. I was so ignorant—"

"But you weren't *trying* to be ignorant. You just have the dream most of us have, a life partner, children…" Bryn's voice was undeservedly kind and held that note of placid resignation that had chaffed him before. He was suddenly extremely glad that all of this had come up now, on day two of their acquaintance— so he could nip it in the bud right away.

"Listen to me," he said, reaching out and gently taking her hands in his. She stared at him. "I'm so sorry my joking comment about marriage and kids was like acid in a wound."

Bryn's mouth flew open and Sean could almost hear her objection or polite lie that it was all right. "Let me finish, then I'll hear you out."

She seemed to deflate, shrinking away from him, even though he still held her by one hand.

"I really like *you.* Maybe for some people not being able to have kids would be a big issue. I get that biological urges are a powerful thing—"

"Are you saying you don't want children?"

"No, I—"

"Exactly—and I always did too. Never imagined otherwise, in fact. So yes, I'm sensitive about it because I'm not in any position to make my own dreams come true, let alone anyone else's. I'm different, *defective*—even my own family thinks so—and I'm sorry if you don't think it's a big issue, but I do. I..." Her voice petered out, then took on new strength. "I can't date someone, chance falling in love, risk all that pain... Maybe it's selfish of me to be so self-interested, but I just can't be not enough for someone, not ever again."

Sean was so stunned by Bryn's flawed view of herself—that she was only of value in a relationship if she could be some sort of brood mare—that he didn't know what to say. And then she was practically pushing him out the door.

"It's almost three. Your cabin should be ready."

"But—"

"I'm sorry, Sean, I really am. I thought I could talk about this, but I can't. I don't want to. It hurts too much."

What could he do? Force her to talk to him when she didn't want to? When it would, in her own words, *hurt her*? He left, sick at heart, feeling like a failure for not figuring out the right thing to say, the way to fix how Bryn saw herself and him—and *them*.

Two-bedroom Rainbow cabin, his for the week, was a wonderful blend of modern yet rustic, but he spent a restless evening, unable to enjoy it. The dinner he made with groceries he'd gone to town for after picking up his keys at the office went uneaten. All he wanted was to show Rainbow to Bryn, to see delight shine in her soft eyes, to have her fill his empty spaces with her kind little deeds and frequent laugh.

It was still early, just before eight p.m., when the idea hit. So he wasn't great at expressing himself with words—no surprise there—but maybe there was a work around. He was, after all, very good with events, big and small. He bundled up, made sure he had his wallet, and jogged over to River's Sigh B & B's office. It was closed for the night, but he took the chance on appearing rude and knocked on the door to the main house.

After apologizing for disturbing them in their off

hours for the second night in a row, Sean ran his plan by Jo and Callum. They gave him enthusiastic, smiling approval, and he burned back into town in his rental car, hoping to catch the stores before they closed, a man with a new mission.

Chapter 13

BRYN AWOKE SLOWLY, LUXURIATING IN the heavy cotton sheets and fluffy duvet, yet aware, even on the brink of consciousness, that she'd liked the bed better the night before. The night Sean had shared it with her.

Just that tiny thought made her tingle all over with tactile memories: the sensation of his limbs tangled with hers, his skin so rough against her smooth softness, the pressure of his mouth and—

She bit her lip, practically rocking on the mattress, as she relived his erection pressing against her through his boxers. Frustrated, she rolled over and tried to force herself back to sleep—but failed.

The dim blue light streaming through the window could be from a midnight moon shining on snow or from early dawn. It was impossible to tell which.

She shoved a pillow out of the way so she could see the bedside clock. 7:33. Not too early to get up, but early enough that it would make for a long solitary day. If only she could've slept until noon. Yes, it was a terrible attitude, but she couldn't help it. It was December 21st. There were four more sleeps until

Christmas, then seven until New Year's Day when she had arranged to check out. That was a long time to holiday alone. Maybe she'd hang tight until Boxing Day, then head home and get some stuff done around her condo before she returned to work.

When was Sean due back to work? Was he staying through until the new year too, or—

Good grief! Could she give it a rest? Bryn mustered energy she didn't feel and climbed out of bed. Steve heard her and zipped into the room, bouncing with glee as if to say, "You're alive, you're alive."

He was impossible to be grouchy around and Bryn smiled a little. "Good morning to you too." She let him outside for a few minutes, then called him back and filled his dish with kibble she'd picked up at the grocery store after she'd forced Sean to go "home" to his cabin. Steve happily crunching away, she hit the shower. She took her time moisturizing and applying makeup, not because she might bump into Sean, she assured herself, but because she had time, so why not?

It was 8:05 when Bryn told Steve she wouldn't be long, then opened the cabin door and stepped outside. She was early, but not too early. Breakfast would be officially underway. She shoved her gloved hands deep into her pockets and hunched down in her coat, so its collar shielded her face and damp hair from the biting cold. She'd only taken three or four steps along the path when she became aware of her surroundings—and totally froze.

What on earth? An army of snow people—okay, admittedly a pretty silly, fun army, but still an army— posed along the path at intervals, big male looking snowmen, tiny child snowmen, lady snow folks... even a tiny snow dog. They all sported cheery holiday garb, toques and scarves, aprons or vests—and every single one carried a poster board sign with a personal message to her.

"Beautiful Bryn, be my skate date?" read one sign, and Bryn noticed the snowman had real ice skates slung over his snowy shoulder and hockey sticks for arms.

Another sign, held by a snow woman holding a huge ceramic mug, said, "Coffee's on, sweet but no sugar Bryn—but I forgot cream. Come by anytime— and bring cream!"

Hardly able to believe the sweet, silly scene before her eyes, Bryn meandered along the path, as sign by sign, snow creation by snow creation, Sean invited her to accompany him to each of the various activities on River's Sigh B & B's Christmas schedule.

It must've taken him all night and where had he found all the props? One ball cap sporting "farmer" snowman stood in a small pile of straw, carried a pitch fork and had a large blowup horse by his side, for Pete's sake. His sign read, "Hey, Bryn. Please don't say no to the hay ride, eh?" It was crazy. And hilarious. And... awesome.

One of the snow people near the end of the line had

a tell-tale yellow stain midway up his base. Bryn suspected Steve immediately and the thought that he'd christened Sean's work before she'd even seen it made her laugh. On a less romantic note, it reminded her to scan the path and surroundings for poop. Steve tended to have an evening constitution, however, and this morning proved no different. She was happy not to have to scoop and run back to the cabin or show up for breakfast with a poop bag in hand.

The last snow person wore a sweater like the one Sean had worn on their trek to find River's Sigh. He had blue stones for eyes and was holding a large yellow envelope with her name on it. Something on the ground at Snowman Sean's feet caught her eye. A toy truck was lodged on top of a chunk of wood that looked like a log, half buried in snow. A tiny sign beside it exclaimed, "Dammit!"

The guy was too much. This was almost… insanity. She couldn't stop smiling though. She reached out, grabbed the envelope and found a note inside.

Dear Bryn,

I can almost hear what you're thinking: This guy's a lunatic.

Sean's words were so close to what she'd literally thought that she laughed out loud.

But before you write me off (or call the police), let me explain the thoughts behind my madness. I had a great time with you and will always remember you fondly, whether you decide to see more of me or not. I wanted to do something equally memorable for you, something that would hopefully trigger that wonderful laugh of yours and make your pretty eyes sparkle.

Yes, building all those crazy snow people was a ton of work (thank you for noticing), but I suspect you're used to doing a lot of work for people that goes unappreciated or unrecognized. You're worth doing work for. (Also, I am kind of crazy, so I might as well tip my hand now.)

And regarding our last conversation... I don't know a lot about your ex-husband other than the bare bones of what you told me, but I don't need to know more. If he left you because you couldn't have children and made you feel like you're somehow damaged, he was not good enough for you, not the other way around. (Am I a bad person if I say I'm kind of glad he was terrible, though? If you guys were still happily married, I wouldn't have a chance with you. If I even do have a chance, that is.)

Anyway, I'm not great with words...

I don't know about that, Bryn thought, her eyes welling.

And I can't promise we won't hurt each other, but what if we don't? What if we have a lot of fun... and maybe, just maybe, something more?

Seriously hoping you'll take me up on at least ~~some~~ *all of my signs,*

☺ *Sean*

I can't promise we won't hurt each other, but what if we don't? The question hummed and danced in Bryn's mind, making her heart race and her palms sweat.

She had meant every sad, pathetic word when she told Sean she didn't think she could bear the risk of so much pain again—but maybe there was something worse: letting fear and self-loathing win and not taking a risk for something you really want.

She still couldn't see what Sean saw in her, what attracted him—and who knew? Maybe spending more time with him would reveal that her initial feelings were due to alcohol and Christmas induced silliness. Maybe she was the one who would end it. Nevertheless, she found her stride quickening until she was almost running, reading each cabin's cute little signpost until she found it: Rainbow.

I can't promise we won't hurt each other, but what if we don't? She knew she was beaming as she reached out and knocked on Sean's door...

Chapter 14

SEAN WOKE BEFORE EVEN A hint of sun kissed the navy sky, but he knew it was morning—or hoped it was. For the first time in a long, long time, he couldn't wait to start the day. He was raring to go, in fact. Then he looked at the clock on the bedside table and laughed at himself. Whether he wanted to or not, he'd have to wait… at least for a bit. His crazy snowmen might have done the trick and thawed some of the hurt-caused ice Bryn had wrapped around her heart for self-protection, but he doubted she'd appreciate him showing up at her door pre-dawn.

He stretched out in the plush bed, thinking it was perfect except for one critical thing: it needed Bryn in it.

He grinned, recalling his surprise when she showed up at his door the morning before. A huge part of him, even while he crafted snowmen and made signs all night, hadn't believed she would. But now here they were, officially seeing each other—and with a milestone behind them at that. They'd already survived the first big obstacles in their fledgling relationship: her insecurities and very sane desire to protect herself, and his stupid bumbling, over the top, much too enthusiastic pursuit.

They hadn't touched a lot yesterday, but every look they exchanged and every laugh they shared as they talked and talked and talked felt like a caress.

And their first official "date" yesterday evening? It was like something from a Christmas movie. Callum's athletic younger brother, Brian, who lived nearby with his pretty wife and two obviously treasured stepchildren, had transformed a small pond on his property into a rink, and Jo had arranged an official skating party.

White lights sparkled through the trees and guided him and Bryn and the other guests down a magical path and over a fairy tale bridge decorated with cedar boughs, ivy and branches of red-berried mountain ash. Sean had wished he'd had a notebook, so he could jot down ideas for Christmas party décor, but then Bryn had sighed softly and he was absolutely and thoroughly pulled back to the moment with her.

The pond was a silver mirror in the darkness, sheltered by a massive spruce tree covered in colored lights. It shone down on a full-size Santa sleigh, with gleaming scarlet sides and shiny brass runners. A burlap sack filled the space behind the driver's bench, looking like it really did hold a special gift for every good little boy and girl in the world. Plunged into a snowbank near the sled, a rustic wooden sign read,

"Reindeer Wanted."

On the other side of the small frozen pond, a quaint shed with gingerbread trim, also outlined in white lights, announced itself as Santa's Snack Shack. Sean figured it probably held gardening equipment when it wasn't doing double duty as a hot chocolate and goodies station. A bonfire blazed nearby, surrounded by log benches.

"Oh," Bryn gasped.

"Oh, indeed," Sean whispered back. "But please don't let this be the bar set in your mind for all our dates."

"Too late," she said and winked.

Christmas carols played softly in the deepening night from an unseen sound system, and once their borrowed skates were laced up, Sean stretched his gloved hand out toward Bryn. "May I have this dance?" he asked.

"You may," she twinkled.

They were both terrible skaters, but that only added to the fun.

"You have to pick me up every five minutes," she grumbled lightly at one point.

"Exactly my diabolical plan when I invited you," he'd said in a sinister tone, rubbing his hands together. Bryn laughed so hard she promptly fell again.

At the door to her cabin when they'd returned late, exhausted from using their muscles in a way they normally didn't, Bryn had raised her mouth to his and let him steal the sweetest kiss, tinged with traces of chocolate and marshmallow—and then she'd pulled away and said good night.

"I could stay," he whispered. "I'll be good, I promise."

"Oh, I have no doubt you'll be good," Bryn whispered back, her double entendre obvious in her husky, humorous tone. "It's me I'm worried about."

That was too big a temptation to ignore. "Well, on that note, how can I say goodnight now?"

She rubbed a finger along his bottom lip, snatching it away just as he moved to lightly nip at it. "You know how some people eat a treat in three big gulps and other people savor theirs, saving it, then unwrapping it and taking a nibble, then maybe another nibble—and then by the time they actually let themselves enjoy it, it's so intensely good it was worth the build up?"

Sean caught her wrist and lifted it to his mouth, pressing his lips against the cool strip of revealed flesh between the cuff of her jacket and the top of her glove. "I'm usually all about reveling in every moment and the postponement of gratification."

She sighed very satisfactorily—and even remembering the sound now made him harden.

Sean's mobile chirped, pulling him out of his memories of the night before. He grabbed the phone from the bedside table where it was charging. Bryn's name showed in the notifier, along with a nameless number that he didn't recognize. He stroked Bryn's name, but the patchy service proved useless as ever. The message, whatever it was, wouldn't open. Then he realized that if she was sending him any text at all, she had to be up and about because her phone wouldn't have service in her cabin either.

He leaped out of bed and showered quickly—forgoing a shave because he liked the way Bryn couldn't keep her hands off his rough stubble. As he headed out into the invigorating air, he couldn't believe how this week that he'd dreaded all year—the Christmas season—had become the best time he'd had in years, maybe in his whole life.

Here it was, just three sleeps before Christmas and rather than wishing the time away, he was desperate to slow it down, to hang onto it. He hoped above hope that Bryn was already at the dining hall, waiting for him, as eager for another day together as he was.

Chapter 15

THE SUN WAS SHINING MERRY and bright, making the whole world a crystal-white wonderland, and the wintery air carried the lovely scent of fresh hay. Whiskey and Schnapps, two gorgeous thick-legged cinnamon-colored horses, stood patiently in front of a shiny blue sled. A young family tumbled down from the plump hay bales, chatting excitedly and thanking the driver.

Anticipation thrilled through Bryn. She'd never ridden in a sleigh before—and Steve shared her delight. He romped and frolicked around her and Sean's legs like a dog possessed, and maybe he was. Maybe the Christmas spirit was affecting them both. She'd rarely felt... whatever it was she was constantly feeling the past few days. She couldn't stop smiling and she was so consistently... warm. Sean, the sight of him, the sound of his low, rumbling laugh and the sensation of his hand so often wrapped around hers, kept her in a constant flush of heat.

"What are you thinking about?" he asked.

"Right now?"

"Yes, like right this instant."

Bryn glanced down at their interlocked fingers. Each of them wore only one glove, so that they could have skin to skin contact. She recalled their other, longer bout of skin to skin contact that first night and her face flamed.

"No," Sean corrected. "Now, I want to know what you're thinking *this* instant."

She laughed, Steve bounced higher, and the horse closest to her nickered softly.

Then Callum was there, helping her and Steve up.

"We really appreciate you arranging for us to have our own personal hay ride—not that one with a group wouldn't have also been fun." Sean hefted himself in beside Bryn, then tucked a furry wrap over their legs and made sure Steve was snuggled securely at their feet.

"It's my pleasure," Callum said. "After all, there are hayrides and then there are *hayrides*."

Sean laughed and Bryn shook her head, then adopted a prim British accent. "I'm quite sure I don't know what you're talking about, but let me remind you, Steve, my chaperone, is very strict."

Hearing his name, "strict" Steve popped up and skipped maniacally about on the hay bales.

"Oh yes, he is formidably stern all right," Callum agreed, grinning. "You two haven't missed an activity yet. You're worth a little spoiling. I noticed you signed up for ice fishing too."

"You bet. Wouldn't miss it," Sean said. "It's super fun to be on the sit back and enjoy yourself side of events for once."

"I'm embarrassed to say how much I'm enjoying the pampering," Bryn added. "You and Jo better be careful or you'll be stuck with us year after—" She broke off, a fresh blush burning her face, one not caused by the sensation of Sean's long leg and hip pressed alongside hers. She and Sean hadn't spoken seriously about the future, if they even had one. It was very early days, after all. The last thing she wanted to do was get her hopes way up.

Too late, her brain said meanly.

"I can think of worse things," Callum said, appearing oblivious to her lame, overly eager, transparent hope. He gave Whiskey and Schnapps each a carrot, then stepped out of the way. The quiet, friendly driver, who owned the team, made a clicking sound. The horses sprang forward with light, joyous steps, the bells on their harnesses jingled, and the hay-filled sleigh glided into motion.

"Hey, don't you dare feel self-conscious," Sean whispered, his breath warm on her ear. "I'm already planning future visits here with you too—and if we ever do get married, I'm thinking we'll need to have a winter wedding with silver bells as decorations. They appear to be a theme for us."

Initially Bryn had found the way Sean seemed to read her mind, to know when she was getting nervous or negative, a bit unnerving. The more time they spent together, however, the more she got used to it, even appreciated it.

He wrapped his arm around her beneath the blanket, then slipped his hand up the back of her jacket and hooked his thumb through one of her belt loops. She nestled closer, grateful for the bells, the swish of the snow, and the horses' pounding hooves. All the combined noise might, just might, keep the sleigh's driver from hearing her own racing blood and fevered heartbeat. She was falling too hard, too fast. Was she a total fool?

"Hey," Sean said. "It's not foolish to bask in this."

Bryn gave him a sharp look. Maybe he was a literal mind reader, not just a figurative one. "Hey yourself," she said, intentionally echoing him. "Come here."

Sean leaned in obediently, and she put her hands around his neck and kissed him soft and slow.

"Yeah," he said when they finally broke apart, "I feel like that too. Exactly."

They burrowed deeper into the blankets and Steve jumped onto Bryn's lap, then demanded an ear rub by bumping her hand repeatedly until she complied.

Sean laughed. "It's like he's saying you've given me enough attention and it's his turn."

It was exactly like that and Bryn was happy Sean was the kind of person who found it funny and cute, not intrusive.

The horses picked up speed until Bryn felt like they

were flying. Beyond them, the sun glinted off white-capped mountains, like every summit was studded with diamonds. On either side of them, forests of snow-robed conifers protected them, ancient and serene, acting as a wind break. Above them, the sky—the deep and endless sky—was like a promise. It witnessed all things and experienced every kind of weather, yet remained undaunted and beautiful in every season.

"I never want to forget any of this, not one second," Bryn said.

"We won't," Sean replied. "I promise."

THE TWENTY-THIRD OF DECEMBER CAUGHT Bryn by surprise. How could there only be two more sleeps until Christmas? How could she have already known Sean for four days? How could she have *only* known him for four days? It felt like they had just met—which was basically true—but also like she'd known him forever. And she wanted to know him forever longer.

"I need to go into town today," she announced, helping herself to seconds of something called "Wife Saver" by Jo and "Strata" by Callum, a delicious concoction of eggs, sausage and cubed French bread. "And I should call my mom and dad, see that they got to my sister's all right."

"What a coincidence," said Sean, grinning. "I also want to go to town and I should see if my family is living it up safely in the sun."

"Do you want to go by yourself, or together, or—"

"Together, for sure. If that works for you."

Bryn nodded, ridiculously pleased by the notion of shopping and running errands with Sean, even though, considering the activities of their past few days, it should seem sort of blah. Instead it felt... seductive and momentous somehow, like they'd been teasing their appetites with fun appetizers and now they were moving on to the stuff of real meals.

"And I was wondering... may I take you out for dinner tonight?"

Why, after all the time they'd been spending together, would this be a question that made her face heat with pleasure?

"I'd love that," she said softly—and remembered the dress she'd brought. "Is it okay if we come back here to get ready before we go out though?"

"Absolutely."

Bryn fetched Steve, whom Jo had kindly volunteered to watch while they were out. Then she and Sean each took a few minutes on the office phone.

They drove her car into town, and Bryn tried to be chatty on the drive, she really did, but her conversation with her mother had brought her down. Her mom was happy to hear from Bryn and had apologized for what, after thinking about it, must've been a "disappointing surprise." Bryn accepted the apology in the spirit her mom intended it, but then accidentally mentioned Sean—and called him "really nice."

"Oh dear," her mother said, like Bryn had said she'd contracted walking pneumonia or something. "Have you told him, this Sean person... your... condition? I hope you don't get hurt again."

Her condition. It wasn't like she had some infectious terminal disease—and yes, she had told Sean. But it was also true that they hadn't talked about it in depth, or discussed how it might affect a long-term relationship or possible marriage.

I hope you don't get hurt again. She believed her mom really meant that. She knew she did, actually. What her mother didn't seem to understand was how *she* hurt Bryn. How the way she acted like Bryn's being hurt was inevitable because no one could ever love her if she couldn't bear children was a reoccurring wound. It hurt just as much, maybe even more, than Brad's rejection ever had.

"It'll be fine, Mom," she'd ended up saying lamely, then wound the conversation up quickly.

"Bryn? Hello? Hey, Bryn?"

"I'm sorry, what?" Bryn glanced away from the road, met Sean's concerned gaze, and scrunched her nose apologetically. "I'm sorry," she repeated. "I was out of it for a second."

"So I noticed." He patted her knee, then left his hand resting on her thigh. She tried to put her focus back on the road. At least the highway was maintained today—well cleared, salted and graveled. "Are you okay?" he asked a few minutes later.

"Yeah, fine." She fiddled with the heater dial on her dashboard, then sighed and found herself telling Sean about her inner conflicts with her parents and her oh-so-prolific baby-producing siblings. They were almost at the four-way stop leading into the heart of Greenridge when she finished. She'd blathered at him nonstop for almost twenty minutes—no, she'd *complained* at him. How mortifying! She was not that kind of person. Or she didn't want to be, anyway.

"I'm so sorry," she said, coming to a full stop and checking the traffic before proceeding through the intersection. "You must think I'm horribly negative—"

"Furthest thing from it actually." Sean's tone brooked no argument. "And I know I'm eventually going to love your family because they're a part of you and they created you—but I also want you to know whenever they hurt you, intentionally or not, I'm going to think they suck."

Bryn giggled. "Okay... I admit that sounds pretty good."

"I'm serious. I'm sure you're right, that they love you—what's not to love, after all?"

Bryn rolled her eyes.

"But I saw all that stuff you packed for them—and it wasn't just store bought whatever to fill space under a tree. You baked goodies, brought games to build fun memories with, chose gifts that would have sentimental meaning."

Bryn couldn't deny it, but she didn't really see how

that made her a super hero or anything.

"You are thoughtful and kind... and not having children to add to the fray? Who cares? You're still you, whether you procreate or not. The only shame is that they know there's a physical element. Too bad you couldn't really throw them for a loop and say you *chose* not to have kids."

Bryn laughed—bitterly, she admitted it. "They'd never believe that in a million years. I remember pushing a pram with great seriousness when I was just three-years-old. I was one of those lame girls who took care of her dolls like they were living people. I planned how many kids I was going to have—three boys and three girls—and named them, created baby books for them, sewed them new clothes all the time..."

Sean made an odd coughing sound and looked out the window. Bryn felt an old familiar surge of despondency. He did think she was broken and messed up—but then he turned back to her.

"I'm so sorry," he said, his voice husky. "You weren't lame at all—and giving up that dream... it must've been so hard for you. It must've hurt so much."

She bit her lip so hard she felt sharp, white pain. "It did," she said tightly. "It does."

It was a relief to have to focus on the road, to have other traffic demanding her attention.

"We never really talked about the having children issue," he said as they stopped at another light. "I guess because we've just barely gotten together."

"You said you wanted them."

"I think it's more that I, like a lot of people I guess, just always sort of assumed I'd have them eventually. I always knew I wanted to get married. I've always wanted a long, loyal marriage, something my parents didn't get because my dad died so young. Children seemed like a foregone conclusion."

"You can't say you've just magically changed your mind." Bryn spiked the gas a little hard as the light turned green.

"It really, honestly, wouldn't be a deal breaker for me. Even now, so early on, not knowing where you and I are really going to go from here, I can say that. Also, I wouldn't be opposed to adopting."

"You don't care if your child isn't your biological offspring?"

"Nope—but if that's an important factor to you, I get it."

"But how can you be so sure it wouldn't matter? What if you didn't have feelings for the child right away?"

"I've heard that can happen even with your blood children, and maybe for some people it would be a problem." He shrugged. "I know how I feel about my niece and nephew, though—and I think, even if love didn't come immediately for some reason, it would show up eventually."

Bryn kept her gaze fixed intensely on the road, although there was no one in her turning lane and no one directly behind her.

"Meanwhile, I'd be there, being Dad, supporting you and our family. I've always thought the actions of love are more important, maybe more real, than fuzzy feelings anyway."

Shaking her head, overwhelmed with a flood of confusing thoughts, hopes and other miscellaneous emotional mess, Bryn pulled into Greenridge's shopping mall parking lot and found a pull-through spot. "This... is a lot to take in—and a pretty crazy serious talk for the stage we're at in our relationship."

"Yeah," Sean said contemplatively. "I wanted to tell you all this—the stuff about being angry at your family for not valuing you more and the kid stuff—before, like on day one, right when it came up, but it did seem too early."

Bryn turned the car off, but they lingered a moment, seatbelts still on. "And it doesn't seem too early *now*?" She knew her tone sounded slightly mocking and that she was compensating for how out of her depth she felt.

Sean turned to her and his face, which had been so serious and empathetic, split in a wide, teasing grin. His eyebrow rose. "Too early? Now? What are you talking about? In days, it's like our fifth anniversary already. Keep up, woman."

Something light and buoyant went poof inside Bryn. That's the only way she could describe the ballooning happiness. Poof! Sean hadn't said it would be easy to figure out the family thing. He'd even, at his most serious, shown he realized that they might not be a lasting couple… but she believed his words and his unspoken sentiment.

If and when a time to discuss a family—*their* family—ever arose, they'd figure it out. He really didn't see her as defective or broken or somehow less than other women. Her infertility wouldn't be, as he called it, a "deal breaker."

They bought some grocery treats together, planning a little Christmas Eve snack night to take place after their ice fishing gallivant, and purchased a massive round of triple cream brie and a bottle of port to contribute to the River's Sigh feast.

Sean left her for a bit to check on the status of his truck's parts, and Bryn used the opportunity to buy a string of lights and some little bells for the tree they were going to get. Then she came across a fresh flower vendor selling cute little balls of mistletoe tied up with plaid ribbon that she absolutely couldn't resist.

When they rejoined each other, it was back to River's Sigh to get ready for dinner.

Bryn straightened her hair, abandoning her usual ponytail, and wore her new dress—a little black number that she never would've bought in a million years except for her friend Kelli's absolute insistence. As she primped, she actually felt… pretty. And then Sean saw her. He took in the dress's low neckline, plunging back, and flirty skirt with appreciative eyes. Then he gave a low whistle. She felt... beautiful. He wrapped his arms around her from behind and kissed her shoulder, then the back of her neck, then her earlobe...

"We don't have to go out," he whispered against her skin.

"You might not have to, *I* might not have to," she whispered back. "But this dress? It is not a staying in kinda deal."

They visited a little Indian place where they munched on crispy pakora and sipped apple cider while they waited for their main courses: spicy chicken tikka for her, creamy butter chicken for him. And in some weird way, in this unfamiliar town and new-to-her restaurant, hours from her condo, her job and her regular life, Bryn had the strangest feeling of being *home*.

In bed later that night, Bryn thought back over the week and tried to pick out a favorite moment, the one that she'd treasure most, regardless of what the future held. She was surprised to single it out immediately and without question. Even with all the romantic contenders—that sweetly sexy first night, the enchanting walk to the magical pond and skating under the stars, the dreamy hay ride—there was no competition. She prized their conversation in her cramped car above all—and how it freed her.

Chapter 16

CHRISTMAS EVE DAWNED COLD AND clear, and Sean couldn't bundle up and get out of Rainbow cabin fast enough.

He recognized the euphoric feeling rioting through him, the same way a person can always find a light switch in his own home, no matter how dark it is. He was falling in love with Bryn—or, more accurately, was already in love with her. He *loved* her. Couldn't imagine not spending every day with her. Was he nuts? Possibly. Did he care? Not one bit.

He whistled as he took the trail to the parking lot. There wasn't a soul to be seen by the van, however. He'd beaten everyone else in the ice-fishing group to the meet up spot. He was about to jog over to Trout to surprise Bryn when two icy hands slid up the back of his jacket, beneath his shirt.

"Well, hello there, stranger," said Bryn in an exaggeratedly throaty voice. His heart thumped with happiness as he turned to greet her.

"Hello there yourself—and hey, don't go away." He caught her hands and slid them back under his clothes so they rested just above his belt.

"Mmm," she said. "You're very warm."

"Am I?"

She nodded and rubbed her palms up his obliques, then over his chest. He took her hips and pulled her close, trapping her arms cozily against his body.

"I think I should return this cold-fingered favor—"

Bryn squealed and tried to squirm away. "I don't think so."

"Oh, no?"

"No."

Her hands were slowly warming, and he continued to hold her close. "How about a kiss then?"

"Well, maybe just one."

"Just one, really? We'll see." Sean had just lowered his mouth to Bryn's sweet, chilly lips when someone coughed behind him. He and Bryn sprang apart like teenagers caught necking—half embarrassed, half resentful.

"Sorry for the interruption," Jo said cheekily, not sounding sorry a bit. "But this is a working holiday."

"Rats, I guess we'll have to settle with a plain old 'good morning,'" Bryn murmured.

"There was nothing plain about that greeting," Sean whispered back, his racing libido in full agreement.

Together they helped Jo and Callum load the B & B's twelve-passenger van with rod carriers, tackle boxes, and insulated lunch kits, while bit by bit the rest of the wannabe fishermen and fisherwomen trickled over.

"No chaperone today?" Callum asked at one point.

"Not a one," Sean said, winking.

Bryn blushed. "I think a full day outside would be too cold for him."

"Yeah, probably," Callum agreed.

They all piled into the vehicle and in no time at all they reached a pullout on the highway and started hiking to their destination, a small lake Jo called a "trout gold mine."

Carrying rods, an insulated lunchbox, and a water-proof blanket provided by Jo and Callum, Sean and Bryn set out behind the rest of the group, keeping up at first, then slowing their pace. Heck, it wasn't like they'd get lost if they fell behind. The trail of boot prints would be impossible to miss.

The path narrowed and forced them to tramp along single file, but Sean kept turning to sneak glances at Bryn. Every time he did, she grinned, and her gray eyes were so soft and shiny, so *happy,* that Sean wished they could pause the moment, hold onto it, forever.

"We're almost there," Jo called from ahead. "When you get to the big cedar, turn right. You'll see our spot soon after." She disappeared around a sharp bend.

Sean had wondered how he and Bryn would distinguish the "big" cedar from all the other big cedars they kept passing, but when they arrived at it, they knew it was the one Jo meant, no question. It was easily ten feet in diameter, with massive branches that had maintained a tiny wedge of sheltered earth at its base, despite the snow covering everything else.

He set his rod down and caught Bryn's arm before she walked past. "Wait, I have an idea."

"Oh yeah?"

He unrolled the waterproof blanket and spread it at the base of the tree. "I know you were really disappointed that you didn't get to kiss me this morning—"

"Oh, I was, was I?"

Her smile was just so dang cute, but Sean managed to nod soberly. "It was super sad, actually."

"Well, it *is* really sad to be sad."

Sean grabbed the rod and lunchbox she was carrying, put them by the tree, then pulled her down onto the blanket.

"This must be some kiss you're planning," she said coyly.

He waggled his eyebrows.

"Well, in that case…" Bryn repositioned herself, so she was on his lap, facing him, legs wrapped around his torso.

Sean's humor turned immediately into arousal, as all his blood pumped to the spot beneath her weight. "Now this is the kind of fishing I could really become a fan of."

Bryn smiled and leaned in, pressing her mouth to his and tasting of cinnamon lip gloss. He kissed her back, liking the sensation of their cold lips becoming warm, so warm. Then he slipped his gloveless hands up her shirt, mimicking the way she'd caressed him earlier. Bryn shivered and bolted upright when his cold fingers connected with the soft bare skin on her stomach. The movement made his groin twinge.

"Brrr," she breathed.

He shrugged and grinned, feeling a bit wicked, loving that he could watch her face and eyes—which widened—as he sought her bra's clasp, nestled between her firm breasts. Freed from their cotton and lace restraints, they were soft and heavy in his hands.

"Like I said earlier, I thought a little payback might be… fun."

She started to speak, but interrupted herself with a sharp inhale when his thumbs found her erect nipples. Her teeth sank into her lower lip as he continued to play.

Slipping one hand free, he reached for a bit of snow, then retreated to the warmth of her again—and added the slippery coldness to her increasingly hard nipples.

She yipped softly but her eyes closed in pleasure, and Sean strained against his jeans.

"*Too* cold?" he whispered. "Want me to warm them up?"

Bryn's eyes flashed open. Her pupils were huge. She darted her tongue across her lips, then nodded, keeping her gaze fixed on his. He unzipped her coat, then her sweatshirt, then gently pushed her tank top up. Her watching him was the hottest thing.

He let out an involuntary groan at the sight of her ivory breasts with their aroused, dusky peaks. A wave of goosebumps rose across her skin as the chill air touched her, and Sean felt an echoing prickle along his own flesh that had nothing to do with the cold.

"You are so beautiful," he said raggedly, then lowered his head to her breast.

She made a tiny noise and raked his hair with her fingers. When his mouth closed on one of her perfect, hard jewels of a nipple and his tongue dragged a warm wet circle around it, she gripped his scalp tightly with both hands.

He could feel her consciously trying to not be too loud. "They're fishing. They won't hear us."

At the word "fishing," her expression changed. She clapped her hands over her breasts and massaged them in slow, soft circles. Sean thought he'd lose his mind at the sight, even though he suspected she was being practical, not intentionally seductive—wanting to warm her nipples herself before taking them away from him. His sad suspicions proved right when she refastened her bra, tugged her tank top and sweatshirt back into place, and did everything up.

His dismay must've showed because she laughed lightly and put one finger on his lips. "That was quite a kiss, all right—but I'm not getting caught au naturel when Jo realizes they've lost us."

She gave him a consolation peck, then a cruel longer kiss that only revved him up more and climbed to her feet.

"I will get revenge for this, you know."

Bryn giggled, arched one eyebrow, and adopted her posh, very unauthentic British accent. "But of course, darling. I'll be expecting nothing but your very worst behavior."

It was all he could do not to pull her down on top of him again.

He stood too, gathered their gear, and followed Bryn down the trail, in tortured—and completely delightful—agony.

They had just spied the lake, as Jo promised they would, when Bryn shot him a shy look over her shoulder. "It *is* freaky though. Admit it."

Sean was honestly confused. "I don't know... I wouldn't call a little outdoor action *freaky,* exactly. Adventurous, maybe."

"No!" Bryn laughed. "I didn't mean... that. I meant how this—*us*—can be so easy, or how you can already be thinking so concretely about being with me... forever. We hardly know each other."

Sean knew what she was saying. In some ways, it did seem crazy. He disagreed, however, that they hardly knew each other. They just hadn't known each other for *long.* Two very different things. "I was with Gemma for years, yet we never got any closer to each other. We only grew further apart—and we were never as easy with one another as you and I are, not even in the very beginning."

Bryn smiled. "We did sort of click right away, no doubt about it."

"And you and Brad dated for what, a year before you got engaged?"

Bryn nodded.

"Then you waited a year to get married?"

"Well, ten months, but close enough."

"But it didn't save you from having problems or ensure your relationship had what it needed to last, did it?"

"Nope, sure didn't." Bryn laughed a little.

"So what's the problem with me feeling sure, so early, that you might be the woman—the only woman—for me?"

Bryn looked down for a moment and when she glanced up again, her eyes were so open, her hope and sincerity so transparent that Sean's breath caught. "It's just that I don't want us—if we do end up together that is—to ever... end."

Sean took Bryn's free hand and squeezed softly. She was doubtful—because she was sane—but she didn't seem fazed by his bringing up marriage. In fact, she was talking about it too.

Finally, he found his voice. "That's why I feel so sure. That's exactly why. Because we want the same thing—a love that lasts. I'm sure we'll have some hard times, but if we share the same mindset, that we want to be together, that we can't imagine being with anybody else, we're going to be fine. In fact, we're going to be *great*. Hypothetically, that is—like if I was dumb enough to be bringing up marriage this early in the game."

Bryn grinned and shook her head, then her expression turned serious. "Is this a game then?"

"Absolutely—but we're on the same team and we get to call all the shots and make all the rules."

Bryn laughed. "Good game."

"There you guys are," Callum called, suddenly appearing around a trio of bushy pine trees. "I was about to come searching."

"Yes, here we are," Bryn agreed brightly. "In the flesh."

Sean bit the inside of his cheek, hard, to keep from laughing.

Despite their mutual anticipation of more alone time, they had a lot of fun fishing. Jo and Callum had made sure the lake was frozen solid earlier in the day and had drilled a series of holes with an ice auger, marking each one with blue flags. Sean and Bryn listened carefully to Jo's tips and followed her directions, using 1/16 jigs with realistic rubber minnows for bait. Apparently if they jerked their rods up and down periodically, it would keep the jigs moving and imitate a lively snack—something trout couldn't resist.

Jo also pounded in a couple of rod holders near Sean and Bryn's hole in the ice and showed them how to insert their rods, if they wanted a less hands-on experience.

"More silver bells," Bryn exclaimed as she examined the setup, flashing Sean a private smile.

"Exactly!" Jo said, misunderstanding her excitement. "They'll jingle if a fish strikes. If you hear it, jerk hard on the rod to set the hook."

Sean grinned. "Oh, the hook's set. Totally. Don't worry."

Confusion then comprehension crossed Jo's face. She laughed. "Okay, stop. I've heard enough. You'll do fine."

And they did. Opting to hold their own rods, despite the pretty bells, they each caught two fat little dollies.

"How fitting," Bryn said laughing. "We'll eat trout in Trout."

Sean groaned good humoredly.

SEAN WAS ON THE FLOOR, leaning against the couch, with Bryn nestled in the V of his outstretched legs. Her back rested on his chest and his arms held her in a gentle loop. He could've sat like that forever. They watched the fire together in comfy silence, mesmerized by the flames and feeling the effects of a whole day spent outdoors, followed by a good meal, and endless conversation and laughter.

The little pine tree he and Bryn had fetched together sparkled in the corner, decorated with popcorn and fresh cranberry chains, plus one small string of lights and some tiny silver bells they'd bought in town.

Steve approved of the yuletide addition and had deserted his chair in favor of curling up beneath it. He looked like a stuffed toy, complete with a new red satin bow around his neck.

"I can't pick a perfect moment with you. Each one just seems better than the last," Sean whispered, reveling in Bryn's soft vanilla scent. It was so *her*: sweet, homey, delicious. He rubbed his hands over her jersey tank top, adoring the sensuous swell of her stomach. Then he cupped her breasts—their image still burning in his mind—and pulled her even more firmly toward himself.

"This okay?" he asked, pushing her silky hair off her neck with his chin, then kissing the spot where her neck melded into her shoulder.

"Mmmhmm." She lifted her chin, so more of her throat was exposed to him, then put her hands over his, which were still on her breasts, and arched her back. "So nice I can hardly stand it."

He agreed—until she moved suddenly, rotating to straddle his hips, and started to kiss him, deep and slow. Then it was even… nicer. His fingers found the soft waistband of her flannel sleep pants and played beneath it, stroking the velvet curve of her lower back where it flared into the voluptuous half-moon of her bottom.

She made another low "mmm" sound, and Sean was reminded of the noises she'd made the first time they kissed—and the ones she'd made earlier that afternoon. He gripped her hips and rocked her back and forth against him, wanting to hear that noise again, wanting to *make her* make that noise again. It was agony trying not to think too much about all the other sounds he wanted to draw from her—all the things he wanted to do to make her shriek and groan and purr. They were both committed to moving slowly on the physical side of things—and apparently equally committed to driving each other crazy while doing so. He loved it.

Sean had just realized that he really needed to change their position for his own sanity when there was a loud knock on the cabin's door. Bryn startled and pulled away from him, eyes wide, lips parted slightly, like someone awoken from a dream. His heart raced at the unexpected intrusion of the outside world, too.

Another knock sounded. Bryn removed herself from Sean's lap and went to answer it. He was immediately chilled by her departure. Steve roused himself from sleep and whined.

"Hello?" she said, opening the door a crack at first, then slightly wider. "Uh, yes, he's here." Bryn motioned for Sean to come, but took a step back from the entrance. "It's Jo. For you," she mouthed, more breath than volume.

He nodded and went to the door. "Hey, Jo. What's up?"

"I'm really sorry to bother you guys, but a woman just called the office, insisting she needs to talk to you, that it's important." Jo hesitated a moment. "Do you mind coming to the office to take the call? She was adamant that she'd hold."

"Of course, of course. Thank you." Sean was already shoving his feet into his boots, his heart pounding. If his sister or mom was calling all the way from Mexico this late on Christmas Eve, there must be something wrong. He hoped no one was hurt—

He turned to Bryn, "I'm sorry—"

"Don't be silly. Go."

"I'll be baaa-ack," he said, trying to joke away his stress with a terrible impersonation of Arnold Schwarzenegger in *The Terminator*.

Bryn smiled, but he could see she was worried too. "Of course—now get."

Sean ran the whole way from Trout to the B & B's office phone. He picked up the receiver, panting with anxiety, not from exertion. "Hello? Hello?"

"Sean? Is this you? Why didn't you take my calls to your cell? I rang and rang. I had to contact your *mother* to find out where you were."

Sean was so fully expecting to hear his mom or Marnie that for a moment he didn't recognize the caller.

"Gemma?" he said after too long a beat.

"Who else would it be?" she said snappishly—or maybe it wasn't snappish. Maybe he'd just become used to Bryn's mellow, low-key, never in a hurry manner.

"Sean?" Gemma drilled him.

"Sorry, I don't have good service here, and your name didn't come up on any calls—"

"I changed my number."

"Okay... so what's up? It's been months. I wasn't expecting to hear from you."

"I wasn't expecting to have to call you either," she said, then rushed on, oblivious to what her out of the blue call might do to him, only able to see, to consider—perhaps understandably, he thought—how her subject matter affected *her*.

Meanwhile, he struggled to keep up with the barrage of nonsensical words. Gemma couldn't be saying what he thought she was. She couldn't expect what she seemed to be suggesting—

But she was. And she was.

As she continued her blue streak of plans and expectations, without waiting or asking for even the slightest reaction or response from him, Sean collapsed into a black leather chair and closed his eyes. His shoulders shook as his new shiny hope and tender love crashed around him.

He had no idea how long he sat alone in the empty office, holding the now dead phone. Minutes? Hours?

A door opened and closed again. Then he heard

Bryn. She had come to get him. The pain of it was excruciating. "Sean? Are you all right?"

Her soft voice and the dim light kindled a memory of the first night she'd sought him out, not wanting him to have to sleep on the hard floor. A grenade of grief exploded inside him. He cupped his eyes with his hands. They'd just met. They'd hardly had any time together. This was supposed to be barely the beginning for them, not the end.

He staggered up from his chair.

"Sean!" Bryn's voice was frantic and suddenly she was under his arm, as if trying to prop him up, worried that he'd fall.

"I'm… don't help me," he said gruffly.

"What? Why?"

But he found he couldn't speak at first. Instead of stepping away, however, like he knew he should, he pulled her to his chest, wrapped his arms around her, and buried his face in her soft, fragrant hair.

She held him, patting his back and rubbing it soothingly. Eventually though, she shifted and he was forced to release her.

"What is it? Who was that?"

"Gemma. My ex," he said brokenly—although, of course, Bryn knew all about Gemma already.

Bryn's brow furrowed. "And?"

"Well, as you know, we haven't seen each other or even spoken in more than six months, but—" He had no idea how to continue and faltered. He hated the concern on Bryn's sweet face, knowing it was for him. Her body, arms loose by her sides, was leaned forward slightly, so open and receptive to him—and he was going to hurt her, though it was the last thing he'd willingly do.

"Gemma's having… a baby. My baby. She says a paternity test will prove it, if I have any doubts. She wants us to… try again, to raise him together."

Bryn literally folded. Her chin dropped to her chest. Her shoulders bowed. Her arms clutched her stomach as if she'd received a physical blow and she huddled over, bending from the waist.

Chapter 17

STEVE WHINED AT BRYN'S FEET, anxiously following her around the cabin as she took down all the decorations, piece by piece, crushing some, throwing others in the trash. Then she put all the stuff for her family out of sight in the big kitchen cabinet. She. Was. An. Idiot. She'd only known Sean for a pittance of time. How, how, *how* could she feel like this at his news that he was leaving her?

And *of course* he was leaving her. She'd never really had him. They'd been playing pretend and she'd been a fool to hope. And an even bigger fool to believe those pretty things he said about not necessarily needing a family.

Now he would have one. Without her. And the worst part? She couldn't even be furious with him, only heartbroken. If he was the kind of man who would just ignore the news he was going to be a father, regardless of when or why he and the mother had broken up, he wouldn't be the guy she found so attractive, so honorable, so easy to—

The thought she could hardly bear to finish

shocked her, but also summed up the worst of it. Somehow, in a mere week, she had come to love stupid Sean Carson.

One last decoration hung above her head out of reach, swinging lightly as if to mock her: the ridiculously hopeful ball of mistletoe she purchased on her shopping excursion with Sean. Bryn grabbed a broom and knocked the taunting greenery to the floor, then opened the cabin door and threw it out into the dark night.

She wanted to go one step further—to take the broom outside and destroy every one of those stupid sweet snowmen, but she'd overheard a couple of children visiting River's Sigh saying how "awesome" they were. Decapitated snowman wouldn't be very merry, and she didn't want their Christmas morning to be disturbing.

She closed the door with a quiet calmness that belied the sorrow and disappointment raging through her. Then she poured herself a mugful of port. It wouldn't be missed by Jo and Callum—and she wouldn't be attending Christmas dinner the next day, no how, no way. Knowing sleep was futile, but hoping for its sweet oblivion regardless, she retreated to the lonely bedroom.

Bryn was right. Sleep refused to come, even when her first mug of port became a quickly drained second one. She sat wide awake in the darkness, wrapped in a shroud of blankets, reliving every moment with Sean and replaying their many conversations and his kind, genuine words. And sometime in the later hours of the night, she had an epiphany.

She had been foolish in the years since Brad ended their marriage. Instead of focusing on all the ways she felt she didn't measure up and was a "failure," she should've concentrated on all she had to give: love, kindness, loyalty, pleasure…

It hurt like heck that Sean had triggered this realization and awakened all this hope and desire within her when he wouldn't be on the receiving end of her new awareness, but she wouldn't continue to let disappointment, bitterness or low self-esteem keep her from living life to its fullest.

She didn't think she'd ever "get over" Sean, so to speak, and she didn't want to. She wanted to remember the wonder and joy he'd kindled, and she vowed—raising her empty mug in a toast for emphasis—that she would remain open to the possibility of love and change and surprises.

Chapter 18

THE RENTAL CAR WAS PEPPY and the road was heavily salted and scraped down to almost bare pavement. Considering the trip that had gotten him to River's Sigh, Sean could hardly believe how easy it was to backtrack—and with every passing kilometer, he felt sicker and sicker with himself. With what he'd done without question: fallen into his old pattern instantly, pretty much asking how high when Gemma said "Jump."

Why had he caved to Gemma, without a second thought? Yes, he believed the child she was carrying was his because Gemma was a lot of things, including smart. She wouldn't bluff about something so easy to disprove. On the other hand, now that he had experienced being with someone who brought out—and appreciated—the best in him, he saw Gemma's demands in a whole new light.

She had insisted that talking in person couldn't wait until after Christmas, but even that was a familiar emotional trick. He'd been pulled in by her urgency. Again. After hours of driving and getting to process things, however, he realized it *wasn't* an emergency. She had known she was pregnant for almost eight months, but hadn't felt a need to enlighten him—had probably been trying to wrangle a way to get Marcus back the whole time and only called Sean when she'd given up. He could take some time to think. He pulled over at a 24-hour gas station on the highway, got himself a coffee and settled into a booth.

What was he doing? No, better question: what was he going to do?

He wanted to be with Bryn, but what bothered him more than being parted from her, was the fact that he'd hurt her badly. The knowledge cut so deeply it felt like he was bleeding internally. But even if he didn't have a chance with Bryn, or, to be precise, no longer had a chance with her (and who would blame her?), going back to Gemma was the wrong decision.

Right now, Gemma felt vulnerable—or maybe she did. More likely her ego was bruised because this Marcus guy jilted her, before he even knew that it wasn't his baby. She wanted someone to make her feel better, and Sean fit the bill. He was a known entity, dependable, controllable… or he had been. It's always easy to manipulate someone who actually gives a damn.

Even the way she'd proposed getting back together had been telling. "So that's that. With Marcus out of the picture and my, *our*, baby due soon, I thought you and I should give it a shot. Try, at least."

No word about love. No apology for how she'd ended things, or for not telling him she was carrying his son until the little guy was almost ready to step out into the world. Not even a pretense of remorse for cheating.

I thought you and I should give it a shot. Try, at least.

Bryn's guileless gray-eyed gaze filled his mind. Then her tenuous smile. He heard her voice, with its heart-on-her-sleeve hope when he'd said he didn't know if he needed kids, that being with the right person was more important. "Are you sure?" she'd asked.

"I'm sure," he had said. And he was.

He stood up and left, leaving his coffee where it sat, along with a five-dollar bill. Back in his rental car, under the glaring light from the gas station sign, he pulled out his cellphone and turned it on. Five full bars of service—the only reason he was grateful to not be at River's Sigh B & B at the moment.

It was after three in the morning, but it couldn't wait.

She answered on the first ring and didn't sound groggy in the slightest. "Where are you?"

"On the highway, but I've changed my mind. I'm not returning to town right away. I have obligations here."

"You have *obligations*? There's something more important than the birth of *your son*."

"Easy on the drama, Gemma. You already told me you're not due until the end of January."

She snorted impatiently, and he sighed, genuinely sad. Unlike Bryn, Sean hadn't spent a lot of time daydreaming about kids—yet if he had, he would've assumed their births would be a source of joy, of celebration. Never in a million years would he have thought of himself as the kind of man who would willingly choose to not stay with the mother of his child. Then again, he'd always imagined something different between him and Gemma than what was.

He recalled all the times she'd declared it was over and had kicked him out or left herself. He re-heard the abuse she'd hurled at him.

His mind flashed on the final lesson, Marcus— though perhaps there'd been other men before Marcus that Sean just hadn't known about.

And then he imagined their child having to watch the same horror show and certainty welled deep in his gut. Being a stable, solid father was the best thing he could do for his child. He would be someone his son could always depend on, always go to or stay with, regardless of what went on with Gemma.

And in keeping with that, he was going to do the best he could for himself, too. He hoped—oh man, how he hoped—that Bryn would forgive him and keep seeing him, but whether he got to be with her or not, going forward, he would live by his principles and ideals, even if it meant being alone.

Sean spoke gently. "Gemma, I'll always be there for our son and for you as his mother, and I hope we can arrange some sort of custody agreement that suits us both. I realize while he's very young, my visits might have to be short—"

"What?" she asked, like there was something wrong with their connection—and yes, of course there was. There always had been.

"I'll always support you," he repeated, "financially and emotionally, but we won't be a couple. We're, as you've pointed out many, many times, not right for each other. I'm not what you want or need. I don't make you happy."

"If you want to be part of this kid's life, you better think and act carefully right now." Gemma's voice was blade sharp. Yelling and guilt-invoking comments would come next.

Sean almost laughed. Gemma's go to moves were so transparent now. How had he not seen through them before?

A feeling of lightness moved through him, despite his sorrow over hurting Bryn, his longing for a future with her, and his questions about what was next for him. True strength involved patience and devotion and working to make things better in a lot of situations—but not in every one. Sometimes it also meant letting go of things you couldn't fix, accepting failure and trying to do better in the future.

Whether he was fortunate enough to end up with

Bryn or not, he was free. "I'm already part of our baby's life," he said, "and I'll keep my word to him and to you, but now I need to go. I'll call you on Boxing Day. There's someone I have to see. Right now."

Chapter 19

BRYN MUST'VE FALLEN ASLEEP AFTER all because very late in the night, or extremely early in the morning, a loud clattering noise at the door jolted her awake. It took a second to orientate herself. Then the events of the past evening rushed back, causing a fresh flood of tears that made her aware of how swollen, scratchy and painful her eyes were. She remembered her vow, to be open to love. It would be a comfort eventually, but right now she just felt bereft. She pulled a pillow over her face, hoping the loud person who obviously had some Christmas surprise in store for the *wrong* cabin would just go away. The knocking only continued, however, even more energetically.

Dragging the bed's top sheet with her as an impromptu robe, Bryn stumbled to the front door, ready to send the intrusive knocker on their way, with the reassurance that it was fine, that she didn't mind being woken up. Lie. Lie. Lie.

She opened the door a sliver—and all planned response slid away. She fell back, retreating silently, sure she was having a misery and port fueled dream.

The dream followed her into the living room, however. And mimicked her motions, sitting in the chair as she sank onto the couch. Steve must've sensed all was not right because although he'd slept through the knocking, he appeared now and looked gravely up at her. Then he jumped up onto the couch and wedged himself against her thigh.

Still no one spoke.

And Bryn really wasn't one hundred percent sure she wasn't just dreaming—or having a nightmare.

"Bryn," the apparition said gruffly—and Bryn saw that the tired, sad-eyed man before her really was Sean, not some conjuring of her pathetic mind.

She opened her mouth, but was tongue-tied. Why was he here? It had been agony enough to say goodbye the one time. They shouldn't drag it out—and if he was going to ask if they could be friends? She shook her head mutely. Maybe it was unkind, but she didn't think it would work. The mind was willing, but her flesh—her heart—was weak.

"I'm sorry," he said. "I couldn't wait for a more decent hour. I had to know…"

Bryn shook her head again, unable to be stupid enough to hope once more.

"I should never have left. I should never have let you think, should never have even hinted at the notion, that I would ever leave you—unless you wanted me to."

Bryn shook her head for a third time. "But what

about—" She could hardly squeeze the words out. "Your baby… your son?"

Sean looked down at his feet, then scrubbed his face with both hands. When he finally glanced up, his eyes were so flat, his expression so miserable, that he was almost unrecognizable. "I know I'm asking a lot, or maybe even an impossible thing… but regardless of what you decide, I won't be going back to Gemma. I will do my best to be a good dad—but alone."

"I—I don't know what you're saying, what you're asking."

Sean moved from the chair and kneeled in front of her. "I'm saying that I know it's too soon and it's kind of crazy, but I love you. And I'm asking if you'll take a risk on a complicated guy with a future that's only looking more complicated. Actually, I'm begging. Will you please take me back, Bryn? Give us another chance. A real chance."

Bryn tried to answer, to say something, but only managed a dry croak—and Sean staved off even that by raising his hand.

"Wait. Before you say anything, you need to know I'm really asking you about forever. It's too early to ask you to marry me—but the question is coming. Or that's my goal. If things between us keep progressing, if you end up feeling the way I do…"

All the pieces Bryn had felt herself break into over the past twenty-four hours knit back together in her chest. A smile tugged at her insides and pulled at her lips. "Before I answer you, I just have to ask… Are you drunk?"

Sean looked startled, then laughed, his eyes full of an emotion that made Bryn's heart squeeze. "I guess that depends on what you say next." He rested his hands on her flannel-clad knees.

"Yes, I'll 'take you back.' Of course, I will. I never wanted to get rid of you in the first place."

"In that case, I confess. I am drunk… Hammered, in fact. On happiness."

She laughed softly, then gasped a little when Sean stood abruptly, grabbing her hands and pulling her up, too. "Come on. There's something we need to do."

"What?"

"You'll see." He tugged the sheet off her, so she wore only her tank top and sleep pants, then put his boots on and motioned for her to do the same. "Don't bother with your jacket. You won't need it."

"What on earth?" But her protest was cut off as he opened the door and pulled her into the brisk, shivery light of Christmas morning.

Dropping her hand as they neared the first snowman he'd built for her, Sean stooped to retrieve something—a bedraggled but still pretty piece of greenery, adorned with tiny silver bells. Bryn recognized it immediately. She flushed with giddy heat as Sean lifted the mistletoe, once discarded, now reclaimed, over their heads.

Her heart lurched as he bent in and kissed her—so

sweetly, so tenderly—and he was right. She didn't need her coat. Her whole body was aflame.

The mistletoe fell with a soft sigh to the snow-packed trail as Sean's arms went around her, pulling her close. The air was cold, the falling snow, gentle—but his lips and his touch were anything but. His tongue claiming hers was as hot as the joy blazing through her heart and coursing through her limbs.

Epilogue

RIVER'S SIGH B & B was as remote and private as Bryn always remembered it—and the light-strung paths leading off in various directions to each cabin were just as magical. In a weird way, her now annual sojourn here always felt like a homecoming of sorts, and she guessed it was. She'd met the heart of her family here, after all.

As if hearing her thoughts, Sean glanced her way from the driver's seat and slid one hand off the steering wheel. Lacing his fingers through hers, he brought their linked hands to his mouth and kissed her knuckles.

"Oh gross, get a room," ten-year-old Drew piped up cheerfully from the backseat, causing Bryn and Sean's seven-year-old twin daughters in the middle bench to chime in concerned unison, "But we already have a room, right, Mom? *We have a room.*"

White-muzzled old Steve stood up from where he was cuddled between the girls and did an anxious stiff-legged jig, as if he was just as fussed by the notion there might not be a reservation as they were.

Bryn stifled a laugh. "Yes, we have a room. In fact, we have more than one. Just like last year. We have a whole little cabin."

There was a shared sigh of almost exaggerated relief from both girls and Anya added in an arch tone, "We *have* a room, Drew."

"Yeah," said Sunny with emphasis.

"I know that, silly. It was an expression," said Drew, but his tone held no malice. He had been thrilled by Anya and Sunny's arrival, which gave him adored big brother status—most of the time.

Listening to their funny kids, Sean and Bryn exchanged a smile, though a tiny part of Bryn couldn't help but ache. Even after two years as part of their family, her daughters' fears still sometimes got the better of them, complicated by mild developmental delays and neglect in their early years. But neither of them horded food anymore, both could sleep through the night, even with the lights out, and each could play alone—didn't scream like they were being burned if they were separated. Love didn't cure all, but it could often cure enough. The words were Bryn's mantra and her prayer.

Reassured, Anya and Sunny resumed bouncing up and down with excitement, oblivious to their mother's concern—as they should be. It was only their second Christmas at River's Sigh, but they remembered it and looked forward to it with as much enthusiasm as Bryn, Sean and Drew.

Sean parked and they piled out into the crisp, pine-scented air. "We'll leave Steve in the warm van until Mom and I check in and grab keys. Anya and Sunny, you two can come with us or you can start walking down the trail."

The girls hemmed and hawed and danced about, excitement warring with trepidation.

"Drew, you should call your mom and let her know you're here before you forget."

Several years back, Sean and Bryn had come for their annual Christmas getaway and found fast Internet and great cell service existed in every cabin, but they preferred to act like the B & B was still out of technology's reach.

"Mom, Mom," Drew yelled. "I'm here. I'm safe!" He ran over and wrapped his arms around Bryn, almost bowling her over.

She hugged him back, then tousled his black hair, so like his father's. "You know what he meant, cheeky kid. Go."

Gemma and Sean continued to be a bit like oil and water in their parenting relationship, but Bryn would always be grateful for Gemma, who, whatever her faults, loved Drew—yet was simultaneously generous toward Bryn, considering another mother to be an "asset" for their mutually adored boy.

Drew grinned and ran off toward the office in real compliance this time.

"I have no idea where he gets his silliness from,"

Bryn joked.

"Silliness? Me neither." Sean put his arm over her shoulders as they walked toward the office. Anya and Sunny made their decision and each grabbed an adult hand, so they were a four-person chain when Jo popped her head out of the office, waving enthusiastically.

"If it isn't one of my favorite families. Merry almost Christmas!" she called.

"To you too!" Bryn returned the cheery wave, and Jo ducked back inside.

"Are you going to phone your parents before we settle in?" Sean asked as they climbed the steps, hands free now because the girls had deserted them in favor of playing with Jo's new puppy.

"Yes, I will as soon as Drew's done." And she would. It would be good to hear their voices and to invite them to come out and take part in this year's winter festivities, along with any of Bryn's sisters, brothers-in-law, nieces and nephews who happened to be around—something that had become an anticipated family tradition.

"I love you, you know," Sean said when they reached the top of the stairs.

"I do know." Bryn planted a kiss on the corner of his rough jaw—Sean still rarely shaved at Christmas—then giggled. "I do have to ask it though... Are you drunk?"

"You know I am."

Sean caught her hand and pulled her back to himself just before she opened the office door. "What?" she asked, slightly startled.

"I just had an idea."

"Yeah?"

"Yeah. Do you think Jo and Callum would watch the kids for a few hours one day, so you and I can do some ice-fishing?"

"So we can do some *ice-fishing*?"

"Yes. I seem to remember an event a few years back, like ten, to be exact, that calls for revenge."

Bryn held back her grin and feigned alarm. "But, sir! You've already taken your revenge over and over again."

"What can I say?" Sean winked and opened the door for her. "I can really hold a grudge."

Thank you for visiting River's Sigh B & B.
"Book" your next getaway soon!

Bigger Things
Wedding Bands (River's Sigh B & B, Book 1)
Hooked (River's Sigh B & B, Book 2)
Spoons (River's Sigh B & B, Book 3)
Hook, Line & Sinker (River's Sigh B & B, Book 4)
One To Keep (A River's Sigh B & B novella)

Visit www.evbishop.com for more titles and release
dates, find Ev on Facebook, or follow her tweets.
She'd love to hear from you!

Dear Reader,

Thank you so much for spending time with Bryn and Sean. I hope you enjoyed *Silver Bells* as much as I did—and that you'll visit River's Sigh B & B again soon. If the series is new to you, check out the other books, *Wedding Bands*, *Hooked*, *Spoons*, *Hook, Line & Sinker*, and *One to Keep*. Also keep an eye out for *Reeling,* coming February 2018, and Aisha's story, *The Catch*, due Spring 2018.

Want to connect? Yay! Please visit **www.evbishop .com**, find me on Facebook or follow my Tweets (Ev_Bishop). On a similar note, reviews really help authors. If you'd be so kind as to leave a rating and a few words on Amazon, GoodReads, your blog, Facebook, or anywhere else you hang out when your nose isn't in a book, I'd be very grateful.

May you never run out of great reads!

About the Author

 **Ev Bishop** lives and writes in wildly beautiful British Columbia, Canada. She is a long-time columnist with the *Terrace Standard,* and her articles and essays have been published in a variety of magazines and journals. Storytelling is her true love, however, and she writes fiction in variety of lengths and genres.

To see her growing list of published short stories, novels, and poems, please visit her website: www.evbishop.com.